T0026065

Numbing Nadine

Numbing Nadine

N.D. Etherly

Art work by Nancy Herschap

Library of Congress Control Number: 2012919234
ISBN: Hardcover   978-1-4797-3286-9
               Softcover   978-1-4797-3285-2
               Ebook   978-1-4797-3287-6

This book was printed in the United States of America.

To order additional copies of this book, contact:
Xlibris Corporation
1-888-795-4274
www.Xlibris.com
Orders@Xlibris.com
122278

For my beautiful and strong sisters,
Dolores Jean and Carolyn Ann

CONTENTS

HALF AND HALF IN PARIS, TEXAS

Nadine's grandfather looked at her and immediately said, "I have nothing against Latin people."

Those were the first words Nadine's grandfather spoke to her. He sat on a wooden bench in the kitchen in Paris, Texas, and looked at her unwaveringly in the eyes. At eleven, Nadine was trapped. These were not the words she had imagined her grandfather speaking to her. She was Avis Janelle's middle daughter. She thought he'd smile, laugh, kiss her, hug her surely, and say how glad he was to see her all grown up. Nothing of the sort. Her grandfather's eyes – blue, frosty blue – never left her face. Was this the man, her mother's father who, on the day she was born, laughed with delight and who, her mother swore, insisted her name had to be Nadine – after Nadine in the Sunday comics, because Nadine's hair was so bushy thick and so midnight black? Nadine rubbed her big toe on the wooden floor, and since she was barefoot, a splinter lodged its way into her flesh. She noticed a drop of blood oozing out and bubbling on the floor. Her grandfather, Jonas Weatherly, didn't notice. *His eyes don't leave my face*, she thought. He seemed to be challenging her for a rebuttal or studying her face for something of her mother. She didn't know if he was disappointed or not. Years later, when she was past the craziness and silliness of a hormone-driven woman making poor choices and stumbling about with her middle-aged, middle-of-the-road coach and after she had wiped the mud, excruciatingly and morosely, from her flesh, she still wasn't sure about that meeting with her grandfather when she was eleven and whether her grandfather liked or disliked her, whether he felt a sense of kinship or a sense of deprecation, whether he felt gladness or sadness, or whether he was simply indifferent. Not so with Nadine's grandmother, Zelma Louise. She'd shoo Nadine and her sisters away like an annoyed housewife shooing yard chickens off the front porch and then go and lie down on the cotton mattress, pat the side next to her, and say, "Come here, dear, sweet Avis Janelle. Come here and lie down with your mother and rest. Just rest, honey. You just rest."

And Nadine's mother would go and lie down by her mother's side, and they'd stay like that: each lying on their side, sighing once or twice maybe but just lying there next to each other. Sometimes they'd talk in low voices – the voices that so amazed Nadine, and still amazed her, especially when she thought of Hamlet, her firstborn, lashing out, whipping her with "You whore!" with real wrath fiercer than the ghosts of Cotton Mather, and how she dropped, like a black widow over pits of burning consciousness. Yet the voices of her grandmother and her mother were never hurried or angry or accusing or judgmental or cajoling or hurtful. They were comfortable voices, like the unpretentious cotton mattress they lay on.

Nadine's big toe smarted. She wished she'd worn shoes. The dirt on the bare floor crept into her toe, stole up her legs, brushed the hollowness in her stomach, squeezed her heart, and settled on her cheeks. She smeared the blood around a bit on the floor with her big toe, drawing a picture. What did he want her to say? Apologize for being half Mexican?

Nadine didn't . . . say anything, that is. With bowed head, she squinted at her skinny alabaster legs with the knobby knees and swirled her bloody toe like a paintbrush about the wooden floor some more. And then she saw herself as her grandfather saw her. In her haste to get out of bed and run to her grandfather, she'd forgotten to put on her pedal pushers! She stood in front of her blue-eyed grandfather, her brown eyes glued to the blood on the floor and, clad only in a gingham blouse and white cotton panties, grimaced.

THE FLOUR-SACK DRESSES

The three little girls jumped out of the car. Each would select one flour sack. Among the various prints were plaids, paisleys, and flowers. Even with the white dust seeping through the coarse weaves of the cotton fabrics, the flour sacks were colorful and vibrant. A fine fog of white flour dust permeated the warehouse.

The three little girls, ranging in ages from eight to eleven, stayed close by their mother's side as they weaved between the rows of stacked bags of flour and cornmeal. Although somewhat on the short side at 5'8" or so, the father was strong and strikingly handsome. With that South Texas bravado, the handsome man walked up to the proprietor and said, "I'll take three of your hundred-pound bags of flour."

The man started to load three of the sacks nearest him, but the mother said to her husband, "Gustavo, the girls would like to pick out the ones with the prettiest prints."

The proprietor stopped and leaned against the desk. The mother and the three girls were already taking in the different colors and the various prints of the coarse cotton fabrics of the flour sacks. "This one is right pretty," the mother said softly and wistfully as she took the youngest and shyest daughter by the hand. Delicate blue flowers danced over a dusty rose background.

The oldest daughter, Carolina, walked from sack to sack. "Com'on," she said to her sisters, "these over here look newer."

The father stood by the counter, near the cash register, and said to the proprietor, "You know how women are, always trying to find a use for something."

He stuck his left hand with the stubbed index finger, which had been cut off in a drilling accident, in his pocket and hitched up his khakis. The perfectly ironed crease in the khakis jerked slightly.

The proprietor – who was tall, skinny, and ugly – watched the short auburn-haired woman with the full figure and the robin-blue eyes guiding the girls from one stack of flour to another stack. He took in her tattered dress. *Looks like it's been washed and rewashed and washed some more. Even has a dishrag appearance,* he thought. All three girls were blessed with coal-black hair and porcelain skin. And what eyes! The eldest had eyes as green as peridot, and the youngest had almond-shaped honey eyes that were large and luminous. The middle one and the most waiflike of the three, and the least attractive of the three, also had the least attractive eyes. They were little: a dingy, dusty coal black.

The handsome man continued, " . . . always wanting to make something." He hitched up his khakis a little impatiently. "Janelle, hurry up. Don't take all day."

The mother flinched a bit and whispered hurriedly to the girls, "Your father's in a hurry. Let's pick out something now. They're all real pretty."

The girls walked up and down the rows of flour sacks, quickening their pace. The proprietor saw the worn shoes and the tattered dresses of the girls, although their dresses were not nearly as tattered as the mother's dress. The waiflike one, the one with the dusty-coal eyes, shot a backward glance at him with something like defiance or disdain, maybe resentment. Her back stiffened. The girl with the peridot eyes said, "I'll take the one with the paisley print, Mother."

"Good, Carolina. That one is nice. Now, Janis, you and Nadine hurry up and make a decision. Don't keep your father waiting."

The shy one with the Egyptian eyes said, "I'll take the one you liked, Mother. The one with the tiny blue flowers."

This pleased the mother. "Nadine, have you decided yet?"

The little coal eyes jumped randomly from stack to stack. "I'll take that one." She pointed to a bright blue flour sack covered with miniature black checks. She turned on her heel and walked toward her father. The proprietor watched the girl. Bony knees jutted out like doorknobs on the skinny little white legs. Her hips were as slender as a boy's, no Rubens flesh on them at all – yet the hips, slender and undeveloped as they were, moved charm-like, like a rattlesnake slithering through the dust. The proprietor jerked his eyes away and looked back at the mother. The mother's dress draped over the large soft breasts and the womanly stomach, accentuating her ample thighs. The proprietor looked at the freshly starched white shirt, obviously new, and the freshly creased khakis of the husband. The waiflike girl with the dusty eyes was heading for the counter.

She walked, swishing her hips like a cobra now, in fast motion. The proprietor thought, *She can't be more than ten at the very most.* Her shoes were run-down too, so were her sisters'; however, the mother's shoes were run-down most of all. His eyes traveled back to the waiflike rat-girl involuntarily, for he was mesmerized by the swishing of the young boy-like hips and the skinny pelvis jutting through the too-tight shift she wore. *Her mother shouldn't let her wear such a tight dress*, he thought.

The handsome man yelled, "Janelle, don't keep us waiting anymore. I've got to get back. Gotta go to work." He glanced sideways at the proprietor. "I'm the tool pusher for the Harkins crew. Working a double shift."

The proprietor nodded. "Pay pretty good, don't they?"

"Yeah, when we work . . . work seven days a week every day until we make a well, then it's no work until they decide to go in and drill again."

The proprietor nodded again in politeness. The girl was almost to the counter. The mother and the two girls came up behind the girl rapidly. The mother's large beautiful breasts moved slightly and naturally under the thin faded-cotton dress. In respect, the proprietor glanced behind the mother at the stacks of flour. Then his jaw fell as his eyes ricocheted again to the mother's breasts. The dress she wore had the same coffee-brown background with small yellow daisy-like flowers sprinkled over it as the flour sack behind her. He realized at that moment that the mother's and the girls' dresses were all flour-sack dresses.

He covered as quickly as he could this sudden realization, but the mother and the girls knew; the father knew too. The mother had, no doubt about it, a quiet dignity; gentleness exuded from her, and she showed no embarrassment. The father strove quickly to the sacks, pointing out the particular patterns that the girls had chosen to the proprietor so he could load them into the shiny aqua-and-white 1957 Chevrolet. The almond-eyed beauty, the youngest and the tallest, looked at him straight in the eyes; it made the proprietor uncomfortable, as if she knew something or understood something of which he had no knowledge. The oldest girl, the green-eyed goddess, stood silently by her mother, holding the mother's hand, her head tilted a little toward the right. She too looked straight into the proprietor's face with no trace of embarrassment.

The proprietor went hastily after the father, trying to avoid the doorknob knees of the skinny one with the swivel hips. Her eyes crackled in anger for a moment, red ants stinging her face, when she'd seen the proprietor glance at her mother's dress and back to the flour sack with the same print. She retracted her steps. The proprietor followed close behind and stood by her father near the stacks of flour sacks.

"We'll take this one with the paisley print." She slapped the flour sack, and little puffs of flour rose in the air. "And we'll take this one with the bluebonnets that our momma likes." She slapped the sack in the same manner, little puffs of flour rising in the air, and added, "We'll take this sack too. This one with the black checks." She slapped this sack too like the others. The little puffs of flour rose high in the air, becoming larger puffs.

Like smoke signals, thought the proprietor. Like smoke signals warning him. He looked at the girl's hand; it was red. Flour, like too much bath powder, covered her hand. She wiped it on the side of her dress and looked at him, then askance at her father, and then peered cautiously, a little frightened, at her father.

But the father only smiled, white teeth gleaming in a wide mouth, and then laughed a little at his daughter. "These are the ones we'll take. Won't have to come back for a few months now."

The girl walked past the proprietor with the same snakelike motion as before, tossing her long black hair. *Which needs washing*, thought the proprietor. She also needed washing. He could smell her, a little girl, not so clean with that dirty-underwear smell that made him all the more uncomfortable. He reached down and lifted up the blue-flowered sack and put it easily in the trunk then hoisted the paisley-print flour sack and placed it neatly beside the blue-flowered sack. The little girl, the waif with the knobby knees, opened the door and scooted into the backseat. Her dress slid up, revealing thin white-as-alabaster legs. She slammed the door hard.

He lifted the checked sack with both hands centering it, abdomen muscles straining, and walked slowly past the window where the Knobby Knees sat, but she had turned her head from him; all he could see was the topmost part of her ear peeking through the tangled long black wavy hair. He threw the bag in the trunk, causing many little clouds of white dust to rise. *Like smoke signals*, thought the proprietor again. He walked past the girl again, sitting next to her sisters. She was fidgeting with the hem of her dress. "Sure want to thank you for your business, Mr. Hernandez. Thank you, ma'am. Good-bye, girls," the proprietor said, crouching down low like a white leopard.

"Good-bye," said the almond-eyed and green-eyed beauties. The skinny one stopped playing with the hem of her dress, crossed one knobby knee over the other, put her elbow on the rolled-down window of the car, and looked out the window. He saw the bony chest move and something like a *humph* come from her throat; the color of ripe pomegranates covered her cheeks.

The father drove off in the immaculate Bel Air and stuck his hand out the window and waved. The proprietor stood there in the middle of the road, next to the mill, with white flour dust smeared on the front of his Levi's outlining his button-fly, and watched the car and the three small dark heads bouncing around a bit in the backseat until it turned east on Highway 359.

UGLY BUILDINGS

"I swallowed a whole bottle of sleeping pills," she stated flatly to her older sister at the door.

The sister eyed her coldly.

"You did what?"

"I swallowed the whole bottle."

"God! You are a nuisance! You're only doing this to make me feel bad about your story earlier."

The young girl did not answer. She turned and went back to the pale green Cadillac and scooted behind the driver's wheel. The glove-white leather interior was serene and peaceful. She let out a deep sigh. Behind heavy lids, the girl focused on the ugly buildings before her where her sister and her sister's boyfriend lived. What shabby, ugly buildings! She closed her eyes and sighed again.

She was seventeen and not so much frightened as tired of finding people so disappointing. Again she sighed and slumped further down behind the wheel. The buildings huddled behind a sign that read The Tropical Lounge and winked at her now and then and would not go away. They were ugly and shabby and dirty.

Her sister came determinedly out of the house behind the bar. "I had to call an ambulance," she said in a peevish tone. She stood by the door of the Cadillac and glared at her younger sister. The younger sister began to feel as ugly and shabby and dirty as the buildings. Shame invaded her face. *So you were raped . . . and spat on . . . and shamed . . . and so you told your sister . . . and so she said you'd screwed some guy . . . and so she hadn't believed you . . . and so Ugly came crashing down on you, and you couldn't put yourself back together again to climb back on the wall . . . and so you took the pills, one by one, very methodically, as if you were counting pearls,* the younger sister thought and shivered in the hot July sun.

Tall and strong by the car, the sister stood, scorn seething in the green cat eyes; neither sister spoke to the other. "The ambulance is here," the older sister said finally in a hard, cold, querulous voice.

The younger sister looked at the ugly buildings once more. They weren't going to fade away. She opened the door and walked to the ambulance and got in. She sat on the stretcher facing her sister and stared past her out the back window. They drove down Clark Boulevard as if they were going to 7-Eleven to get bread and milk.

"She swallowed a whole bottle of sleeping pills," the sister said to the doctor.

The doctor caught the sister's anger with his hands. "Why did you do such a thing?" He gesticulated with real irritation and then, with a confusing Mexican-German accent, he accused, "You young girls are like this all the time. If you want to kill yourself, that's your business. But then you change your mind, and you come here." He swung around and picked up a plastic tube.

"This will not be pleasant." He stuck the tube in her nostril. The girl felt as if she was being raped again. She did not cry out when the doctor crammed the tube in her nostril, nor had she cried out when the boy crammed his penis in her vagina.

She watched her stomach fluids being sucked up and expelled into a stainless steel pan.

The older sister glared at the younger sister. "Is that all?" she asked the doctor.

"Yes."

"Well, let's go," she said.

The doctor lost some of his curtness. "You will sleep a lot for the next two or three days," he cautioned. "Next time, do not do such a thing." He awkwardly touched her shoulder. The young girl said nothing.

"Let's go." The sister jerked her arm and led her away like an angry schoolteacher leading an unruly schoolgirl from the classroom.

The two sisters saw their father standing in the waiting room with Colin. "You need to come with me," the father said sternly. Colin looked uncomfortable.

The older sister said, "Go home with Father."

I am so sleepy, thought the young girl. She yawned. She knew she would not go back to her sister's house, for she could not sleep with her sister's contemptuous eyes stabbing her; nor would she go to her father's home, for she could not sleep with her father's morose eyes questioning her.

She slurred, "I just want to sleep," and took Colin's arm.

Colin said, a little cowardly, "Maybe you should go with your family."

"No," she said and turned to her father. "I will be fine, Father. I just want to sleep."

When Colin took her to his apartment, she lay in his bed, and he stroked her cheek. "Do you want me to hold you?" he asked.

A deep horror and repulsion spurted through her. She shook her head no. She watched him for a while, a funny little man with friends like that boy, and then she fell asleep.

THE NIGHT SHIFT AT WAGNER'S CAFÉ

The girl, all eighty-eight pounds of her, held the paper pad and pencil in her hands and asked politely, "Have you decided what you'd like?"

The man – fifty something, tall, about six feet four inches – looked up from his menu, placed it on the table, and let out a low whistle. "Yeah, I have, and it's not on the menu."

He looked straight into her heavily made-up Elizabeth Taylor-Cleopatra eyes and then let his eyes travel sensuously down the pink uniform Mr. Wagner made all his waitresses wear and then lifted them calculatingly, targeting and violating her breasts with his eyes. Nadine shivered. He had steel-gray eyes – eyes like ice picks.

She stepped back and almost fell. Red anger spread like blood on her cheeks. Noticing this, Marissa, the head waitress, frowned at her. *Be polite to the customers*, her frown warned, for "Be polite to the customers" was the maxim. Unsuccessfully, Nadine attempted to look the man in the eyes, but her eyes jerked about furtively, searching for an escape. She saw Marissa's watchful eyes grow more menacing, so Nadine said as steadily as she could, "We only serve what's on the menu."

The man's cold gray eyes narrowed, penetrating the two inches of foam rubber that transformed Nadine from an A cup to a C cup and, knowingly and decidedly, pulled his wallet from his hip pocket, opened it, and with his thumb, flipped through a thick wad of dollar bills. He slowed the process down so the girl could see that these bills were not one-dollar bills but hundred-dollar bills. The girl felt the little hairs on the nape of her neck stiffen. She looked around the restaurant; several customers were lingering over coffee, so she was safe. She waited. With his fingers, the man strummed the hundred-dollar bills again. Nadine looked intently at the menu on the table.

"I'll have a hamburger: fresh, rare, and juicy," the man said and placed the wallet, belching with the hundred-dollar bills, on the table. Nadine turned the order in and neglected to go back to the customer and ask him if he needed a refill for his drink, knowing that she wouldn't be chastised by Marissa, for Marissa – after spotting the hundred-dollar bills spewing from the wallet – was suddenly obsequious toward the gray-haired man with the ice-pick eyes.

While Nadine waited on the flyboy, Michael Smith, from the Laredo Air Force base, Marissa interrupted in a miffed voice, "He wants *you* to take his hamburger to him."

Nadine placed the man's burger on the table and turned to go back to Michael's table when the man, in a controlled voice, said, "I'm going to leave you a big tip. I like the way you serve me."

"I don't take tips," Nadine flashed back, fiercely and proudly. Once again, the man's ice-pick eyes travelled up and down her body; his eyes rested and lingered on her tattered shoes.

"Sure, you do," he said familiarly.

"No. I don't take tips. Never have. Never will."

The man looked at Marissa who, at the adjacent table, was wiping it clean.

"Nope, she doesn't. Everyone thinks she's nuts. Me too. She won't take nobody's tips," Marissa affirmed. Then she muttered under her breath, "She thinks she's better than the rest of us."

The man sat there for two, maybe three, hours in Wagner's Café on San Bernardo, waiting with his bulging wallet on the table, hoping the girl might come back to his table.

She didn't. Nadine kept a wide berth around him. When the early morning sunlight streaked in through the dingy windows and the breakfast crowd streamed in through the crooked doorway, the man peeled a one-hundred-dollar bill from his wad and placed it on the table, watching to see if the girl might come back. She didn't even glance at him; instead, she stood in the center of the room, waiting on customers here and there. Several minutes passed, and then the man with the ice-pick eyes left Wagner's.

"Look, Nadine! *Mida! Mida!* He left you a hundred-dollar tip! *Cien dolares!* I bet you take this tip!" Marissa shouted with malice and glee, waving the hundred-dollar bill above her head, but Nadine simply shook her head and said again, "I don't take tips."

She placed iced water on the table where a man and his wife, dressed in faded but clean clothes, were studying their menus. They smiled, almost in relief; behind them, Marissa quickly folded and stuffed the hundred-dollar bill in her soiled white cotton brassiere.

In a few minutes, it was 7:00 a.m. Nadine punched out, got into her battered old red Covair, looked around warily, and reassured that no gray-haired pervert was lurking about in the parking lot, drove down San Bernardo until she was a few blocks from the bridge. She turned right onto Farragut Street, pulled up next to a shabby apartment building, and sprinted up the stairs to 8B. Nadine unlocked the door and, after checking the bathroom and the kitchen to make sure all was safe, stumbled over a few "borrowed" books scattered on the floor, collapsed on the worn mattress in the center of the living room/dining room/bedroom, and – as only a seventeen-year-old can do – was asleep within minutes.

After all, she had no worries: a lone but newly-purchased package of bologna was in the refrigerator, a loaf of white bread was on the countertop, a full tank of gas was in the Covair to get her to and from Wagner's, and rent was not due for another three weeks. Life, working the night shift at Wagner's Café on San Bernardo, was simple and good . . . at seventeen.

THE MAN IN OVERALLS

The man, about five feet five inches tall, minced up to the bar. Zach Wilkinson, at six feet five inches, was as tall sitting as the man was standing. Zach is, of course, wearing Wranglers, which smell of Freer dust and dried cow manure, and a frayed old cowboy shirt, the kind with pearl snaps. The short man, about fifty something, is wearing overalls as dusty as Zach's Wranglers.

Zach reaches out his enormous hand and clamps it down on the smaller man's shoulder. "Hey, Jimmy. Sit down. Here. I'll buy you a cold one."

The man in overalls climbs up on the stool next to Zach.

"What can I get you?" I ask and smile, for the man looks tired and uncomfortable.

"Guess I'll have what Mr. Wilkinson's drinking."

"Okay. One draft. Lone Star." I get a cold mug from the freezer and fill the mug with the urine-colored real man's beverage.

"Nadine, this here's Jimmy. Jimmy, Nadine. She's been working here about a year or so."

"Hello, ma'am," he says.

"Hi. You from Freer? I haven't seen you in here before."

"Well, yes'm, I am. But I don't get out much."

Zach tiptoes like a big cat on little soft feet across the wooden dance floor and looks at the forty-fives in the jukebox. "Whatcha wanna hear, Nadine?"

"Doesn't matter. You choose, Zach."

"Nope. I wanna play something you like," he returns.

"Okay. I like Patsy Cline. 'I Fall to Pieces,' 'Crazy' – anything by Patsy Cline. And I also like Merle Haggard. I like 'Silver Wings' and 'Okie from Muskogee.'"

I hear the quarters tinkling down the slot and Zach pressing buttons.

"I played them all for you, Nadine," he says with a huge smile, sweat gleaming on his forehead. "I'll have another one of those cold ones. Get the frostiest mug you can. Want another one, Jimmy?"

"Well, yes. Yes sir. Don' mind if I do," Jimmy says. "Thank you," he says when I place another one in front of him.

Zach winks at me. I laugh to myself. How foolish fortyish men are! Instantaneously, an image of Zach on top of me flashes before my eyes; I can't control it. I am blessedly cursed with an overactive imagination. All these vulgar images flash like neon lights before me. Most of them make me laugh or grimace, some make me hollow and sad, and others are unspeakable horrors. I'm not sure that I don't feel all these impressions when a glaring red image of Zach – naked except for his cowboy boots and sweaty blue bandana, all 350 pounds of fat and some too of muscle – lunge down on me, all eighty-seven pounds of me. I squeak and hunch up my shoulders for a sec and then gain control and smile at Zach with my barmaid smile – my friendly-only (because I am the barmaid, and you are the customer) smile, and you can't climb over the steel wall covered with thorny rosebushes and prickly pear I've erected for myself. This smile, friendly with a steel fence behind it, works well and is necessary. Every man that comes into the Blue Dog, tired and dirty from working too hard and too long in the frying South Texas sun, gets a little light-headed and wishes (oh, I'm not special. I know any girlish woman will do. If not me, then some other barmaid) I'd go home with him and serve him a cold beer . . . without clothes on. Ugh.

When "Silver Wings" plays, Zach asks me to dance, and even with that nefarious image branded on my mind, I – all five feet of me – dance with him. I'm curious.

He is amazingly light on his feet, graceful even, and he holds me, respectfully and a little shyly, at a distance from him; a vertical bridge of about a foot and a half runs parallel to our bodies. We both enjoy the dance. I know he's a little sweet on me, as much as a white man can be for a little half-white/half-Mexican barmaid, but I'm no fool, and I know not to narrow that vertical bridge between us on the dance floor or *off* the dance floor.

We're back at the bar, and Zach gets talkative. "Since you're from Bruni, you ever meet that Williams girl? The one from the big ranch between here and Bruni? Know Wanda Sue?"

"No," I say. "But I know who she is. I've seen pictures of her in the Bruni High School annual."

"Whatcha think about her?" he asked, hunched over his beer and swirling and sifting through the peanuts with his fingers.

A bit of advice: you don't *ever* want to nibble on peanuts placed before you on a bar counter.

"I think she's pretty . . . very pretty," I say genuinely and without envy. A woman, even a girl-woman like me, can be genuine like this with a man. Easy to do when you're not in love with the man.

"Yeah?" he says.

"Uh-huh." I nod.

Of course, I know he likes her – lots, 'cause he's acting way too casual. But I stay on course. "She has this real short pixie cut, has light auburn hair, almost a strawberry blonde, and she's tall," I say. "She is fine. Pretty," I add.

"Hey. I like that. Not afraid to say another woman's pretty," he says admiringly, but I know he says it really so I will continue to talk about Wanda Sue. *It's a little thing*, I think to myself. *Kind of like Gerasim raising Ivan's legs and placing them on the back of his shoulders.* Zach spends too many afternoons at the Blue Dog to have any kind of a private life.

"Well, she *is* pretty. *Very* pretty," I repeat. I'm a little flattered, in spite of myself, and I slide another beer toward him.

His eyes light up. "Yeah."

"Yeah," he says again, a little softly and tenderly for such a Goliath of a man.

After a few minutes pass, I ask, "Were you friends?"

"Yeah," he responds, and then he talks and talks and talks about Wanda Sue Williams with the long legs and the pixie cut and "the freckles sitting purdy on her nose." *This guy's got it bad*, I think to myself. *They'd dated all through high school, then he gets real busy at the ranch, and they drift apart? Yeah. Nice way of putting it. She found someone she liked better: someone slim and tall and rich, probably.*

I need to say something, so I say, "Sounds like she was a real good friend, Zach."

He nods his head, and I hear the forty-five drop, and Charley Pride comes on. And Jimmy – who we've forgotten about but who's listening respectfully to all Zach and I have to say about Wanda Sue and who never pitched in his two cents – asks me, hesitantly, "Can I ask you a question?"

I frown a little. I can't tell you how many times that line has gotten me in trouble. I frown some more. "Guess so."

So this little old man, about fifty or so, all dusty and hunched over, timidly asks – no, humbly asks, "Would you dance this dance with me?"

I hesitate. "I don't dance much," I say, but then I remember the humbleness in his tone, and anyway, I'm tired of standing behind the bar, and now Zach's a little embarrassed about prattling on about Wanda Sue Williams, and that will surely put a strain on the next time he comes into the Blue Dog. I don't particularly want to dance with this little old man. He's smelly and dirty, yet I feel a little sorry for him. So I say okay, and we walk out onto the dance floor.

Anyway, we dance with that parallel bridge between us. It's a slow afternoon. Only Lulu and her husband are in the bar besides Jimmy, Zach, and me. Billy Jon'll be in any minute now. I'm a little uncomfortable. I look toward the door, wanting Billy Jon to come swinging in 'cause I'm Billy Jon's girl. Anyway, he's the only one I leave the Blue Dog with, so I glance toward the door again. It's closed. Jimmy turns me around awkwardly on the dance floor when I get this open-freezer-door chill that runs up and down my spine. I glance over at the bar. Lulu, Jet, and Zach are all staring with hard little wolf eyes at Jimmy and me; I see hate-burning eyes, boring holes into me and sneering at me. I stop before the music stops. I can hear the record sliding back into its slot; it's that quiet.

Jimmy sounds a little scared. "I shouldn't have asked you to dance with me, ma'am," he says, a little hoarsely. We walk back to the bar.

I go to my place behind the bar, and Lulu and Jet turn their back on me and walk abruptly into the adjoining storage room, whispering in ugly tones to each other.

It's quiet . . . so quiet. I look at Zach, perplexed and questioning, but he won't meet my eyes.

"Want another beer, Zach?" I ask.

"No. No, I don't," he spits out.

"How about you, Jimmy?" I ask.

"He don't need any more. You gotta work tomorrow, Jimmy. Time you was a going," Zach says gruffly. "Don't want no drunk ass working for me and Billy Jon."

Jimmy says, "No sah. No sah. I'm going home now."

Zach says, "Me and Billy Jon'll pick you up at six in the morning. You be ready, ya hear?"

"Yes sah. Yes sah," Jimmy says. "Thank ye kindly, miss, for that dance. Ain't anybody ever danced with me before."

I say, "You're welcome."

The chill down my spine gets colder as Zach menacingly snaps, "You run along, Jimmy."

"Yes sah. Yes sah," he says.

A ray of hazy sunlight slips on the dance floor when Jimmy opens the door and leaves. I can hear the hum of the refrigerator behind me and Lulu and Jet unloading crates of beer and soda pop in the storage room. Zach won't look at me. After a while, I pick up a dishrag and polish the counter. There are no more quarters in the jukebox, and Stillness sits heavy with arms crossed.

I look at Zach again. I open my mouth, the beginning of a question forming, when he jerks his eyes up, upper lip quivering, and little drops of saliva pellet my face. "Why'd you have to go and dance with that *nigger*?"

It took several weeks of patience and mincing steps before the frostiness thawed toward me at the Blue Dog. "Anyway, what did you expect?" the locals speculated. "Nadine's not all white. She's shown her true colors. She's gotta have more *Mesican* in her than white blood. Someone said her mother's white. But then the momma went and married a *Mesican*. Nadine don't know no better. Ain't white."

Billy Jon told me a group of men, cowboys, lawyers, and bankers at Price's Restaurant spat wads of tobacco juice on the sidewalk when they discussed that disgusting dance.

It took several weeks for Jimmy to muster up the courage to come into the Blue Dog Lounge again, but I knew he would, and I had my answer ready. After the second beer, he asked me to dance, and I said in a noncommittal manner, "No thanks, Jimmy. I don't dance with anyone but Billy Jon."

Lulu and Jet looked pleased with my answer. I went back to polishing the counter, avoiding my reflection in the heavy layers of wax and cigarette burns, and listened to Lulu and Jet exclaim that I was the best help they'd ever had since they'd opened the Blue Dog in Freer, Texas.

BILLY JON'S GIRL

The first time I saw Billy Jon was just after my eighteenth birthday. I was behind the bar at the Blue Dog Lounge in Freer, Texas. He walked in the door with Zach Wilkinson, a well-known local rancher: a huge man, 300-plus pounds at least. Both came right up to the bar and ordered two Pearls.

"Make mine a draft," Zach said.

"Gimme a longneck," Billy Jon said.

Zach took off his soiled Stetson and put it on the barstool next to him. Billy Jon left his hat on, even when Zach introduced me to Billy Jon, saying, "Nadine, this is Billy Jon. Billy Jon, Nadine."

To this day, I'm not sure what Billy Jon said to me. I *do* know he didn't take his hat off or tip it back or look at me and whistle and say, "You're the prettiest little thing I've ever seen," like all the men who came into the Blue Dog did.

I *do* know when I looked up into Billy Jon's face, I saw the bluest and absolutely clearest eyes I've ever seen in my life. I think I gasped. Still to this day, I'm not sure, but I saw a strong weathered face – a man's face. A face that knew sun and lived life.

Zach said, "Billy Jon's from San Antone. Staying out at the ranch for a couple of days." He reiterated, "He'll be here only a couple of days, and then he'll be gone."

About that time, someone puts a quarter in the jukebox, and Charley Pride's "Is Anyone Going to San Antone" slithers across the dance floor.

"Dance with me," Billy Jon says.

Not even a hello or a nod, just "Dance with me." I look over at Lulu to see if it's all right, and she nods.

Billy Jon eases down from the barstool. I look up, up, up at him. He's six foot two, at least. I think, *I'm only five feet tall and weigh all of ninety pounds.* He reaches for my hand and pulls me toward him easily, naturally, and with his hand resting lightly beneath the nape of my neck, he leads me surely and in rhythm to the music. We are one. I feel his warmth, his sureness, and realize I am not afraid like I always am when men dance with me.

He leads me back to the bar, walks me behind the counter, and is about to let me go when "I'll Waltz Across Texas with You" beckons us, and he pulls me out from behind the counter, saying over his shoulder to Lulu and Zach, "This girl's mine," and guides me with a smooth twirl back into his arms. We waltzed. We waltzed across the barroom floor, oiled smooth with fresh sawdust the night before. We waltzed across Freer and frozen smiles. We waltzed across Texas in that little honky-tonk as if no one else existed in the world. They didn't.

He'd watch me, his welkin eyes following me, as I got frosted mugs from the freezer and filled them with draft beer, tilting them ever so slightly so as not to get too large a head on them, and his eyes followed me as I chatted with customers or waited on tables. Lulu just came out from the backroom and worked the counter or waited tables if Billy Jon wanted to dance with me. Waltzes warm women, and Billy Jon warmed me, wooed me, and won me with those waltzes at the Blue Dog during the hot, sweltering summer afternoons and nights in Freer, Texas.

Zach was right and wrong. Billy Jon stayed a couple of days . . . and then he stayed a couple of more days and then a couple of weeks and, after that, a couple of months. He'd go back to San Antone for a day or so and then in the early afternoons, as soon as my shift started, Billy Jon would come sauntering through the door wearing freshly pressed Wranglers and old Luccheses and ease down on the barstool closest to me and order a Pearl. He drank nothing but Pearls. If the Blue Dog ran out of Pearl, he'd just stop drinking for the night.

I've never seen anything like it then or since. He'd put away ten, maybe fifteen, beers in the long afternoons and keep right on drinking, sitting on his barstool and watching me, sometimes waltzing with me until the Night would say invitingly, "Last call," and then firmly, "It's closing time." And at closing time, I was with Billy Jon. Always.

He wanted me to watch. "You've got to come out with me, Nadine, and watch Jeronimo. He's a fine stallion. He's stamping and raring and lunging even before he gets out of the trailer. Catches the mare's scent." Billy Jon explains and lets out a low whistle, "You really ought to come out to Zach's ranch, Nadine, and just watch that prize stallion of mine."

I shake my head. "No, I don't want to go out to anyone's ranch at this point in my life," I say.

"I'd pick you up and take you out there myself and stay with you the whole time. Would you come then?" he asks. He puts his arm around me protectively.

I snuggle a little closer to him, look up at him, and say, "No, Billy Jon. Not even for you."

He leans down, scoops my chin in his hand and lifts it up, and kisses me long and slow on the mouth.

"Come on, Nadine," he says softly. "Come on," he repeats. "There's nothing like it. Absolutely nothing like the sight of that horse of mine lunging up high into the air and coming down on that mare of Zach's."

He puts his arms behind his head and pushes his pelvis forward, long legs spread wide. *God, he's such a fine cowboy. Such a fine man,* I think. My eyes are drawn to the beauty of Billy Jon: strong, firm jaw; Mt. Rushmore – chiseled features; and perfect symmetry. Even the seams of his Wranglers meet in harmony at the center of his manhood.

I want him to kiss me again. I say softly, "I'd be afraid to go, Billy Jon. I've never been around horses."

"You don't need to be afraid, I'll be there. You'd stay behind the corral."

"Maybe," I say hesitantly. "Maybe then, maybe I might go with you sometime."

Of course, I have no intention of going, but I say it to please Billy Jon.

"Tomorrow?"

"No, not tomorrow," I say. "Lulu wants me at the Blue Dog at noon with her to open up."

"Tuesday?"

"Maybe," I say and snuggle under Billy Jon's arm, and we both watch the moon until it sinks low in the sky, winking and smiling at us. That's the way it was: Billy Jon sipping on his longneck Pearl and kissing me every now and then, and I wishing upon a falling star that Billy Jon would lean over and unbutton my blouse after one of those kisses.

One night, a couple of months later (we're doing the same thing: Billy Jon's drinking Pearl beer, and I'm waiting for the next kiss and already wanting the next one and wondering too if he can smell my scent exuding from my jeans), I reach out and place my hand, rather timidly, on Billy Jon's crotch.

"Whoa, Nadine," he says low. "Oh girl. Oh girl."

I touch him.

"Girl, I haven't since Maureen . . . and she's been gone for over a year now."

"Ummmm," I say compassionately. "Maureen's a fool for leaving you, Billy Jon." But I don't stop what I'm doing, and pretty soon, Billy Jon's unzipping his Wranglers and I'm bending my head beneath the steering wheel of the blue 1960 Chevy pickup.

"Oh girl, Nadine, you're mine," he says later. "You're my girl." He drinks another Pearl, and I swallow an iced-down coke, letting the fizz sterilize my throat.

And that's the way it went. Talk, talk, talk . . . watch the moon rise and sink . . . drink Pearls and cokes . . . kiss, kiss, kiss . . . And then Billy Jon would have his Wranglers unzipped, and pretty soon, my lips and throat would be swollen, and that was that. Then, sometime later, Billy Jon would drop me off and go rambling down Highway 44 in his battered old blue Chevy pickup truck while I unzipped my pants for the first time that night, like many other nights before that, and laid them over a chair before getting into bed and staring at the deep cracks in a none-too-white ceiling. That was the great love affair between Billy Jon, the forty-six-year-old man from San Antone who'd bring his prize stallion to Freer to stud out in the early seventies (or was it the late sixties?) and who'd been dumped by his rich testicle-tearing, smash-Billy-Jon's-balls bitch of a wife Maureen, and me, a just-turned-eighteen-year-old half-white/half-Mexican, little honky-tonk barmaid of a girl, wearing unzipped jeans and foam-rubber bras, who'd dropped out of high school.

One day, many months later, when the smoke in the Blue Dog was a little too thick and life a little too thin, I threw my clothes into my faded jaded red Covair that my father had bought for $200 and given me and left Freer for good and headed, not home, but west to Laredo.

Sometimes I think of Billy Jon. And once, years later, when my husband and I were at the stock show in San Antone, I saw Billy Jon, still wearing freshly pressed Wranglers and holding lightly a Pearl longneck in his hand. I could not stop myself. I stumbled, and I leaned momentarily against Billy Jon, resting my cheek on his chest. He stopped talking to a circle of friends, and his hand found mine and held it fast. "Girl, Nadine," he said and I smiled, smiled, smiled at Billy Jon and pulled away and let the crowd cover my cowardice. I've never seen Billy Jon again.

But god, oh god! Billy Jon could waltz (I'd never waltzed with anyone before him or after him), and his eyes – they were bluer and were clearer than the bluest clearest skies, unmarred even by persistent clouds. And I was tempted, real tempted, when I was eighteen . . . when I was Billy Jon's girl, to waltz across Texas with him.

THE BUS DRIVER

Moving back to Laredo was risky in many ways. I had to stay hidden; someone might recognize me as one of the Tijuana Girls. No longer using my maiden name was a natural cover-up. Yesterday, I'm unloading Hamlet in the handicap zone at Navarro Elementary, and a United Independent School District bus pulls behind me, blocking me. It's obvious the principal has told all bus drivers to make it difficult for me in retaliation for me spouting off about the lack of handicap parking. It's Tino, some thirty-odd years later, sitting behind the wheel, bigger and heavier than he was when he'd come to happy hour at the Tijuana Jail. An enormous black mustache covers his big thick greasy lips. He sees the woman struggling with the spina bifida child; he doesn't recognize me. I keep my face averted.

Tino. So this is Tino now, driving a school bus, and this is I, Nadine Hernandez now, unloading a hurt little boy – my son.

Tino. Yvette. They were a twosome. While Yvette's husband was in Vietnam, Yvette worked at the Tijuana Jail to pass the hours and days until Nick came home. She chased red birds with yellow jackets, smoked weed, and did harder drugs, I'm sure, with Saul and Bill.

Tino. What was his name, anyway? We called him Tino always. Tino started coming into the bar late in the evenings for the last floor show, which was something of a misnomer. We go-go girls all danced about awkwardly and energetically in two-piece bathing suits, and he hit on us all: Ronda, Yvette, and me. He was turned down by all of us consistently until, one night, Yvette swallowed more red birds than usual, was lonelier than usual, was sick of worrying about Nick, and got horny. After that, it was Pablo and Ronda, Tino and Yvette, and Jason and I.

He was obnoxious, always leering at the girls and right in front of Yvette. He'd stare at your breasts and make comments like "I could make you real happy if only you'd let me." Or he'd say, "You need a man, a real man. Doesn't she, Yvette?" And Yvette would laugh, throw back her head, and swallow another red bird.

One afternoon, Yvette and Tino came over to the trailer with a six-pack of beer. We sit in the living room. Yvette is wearing my purple Western vest with no blouse underneath it. The nipples are covered, but that's about all. She has full breasts, wide hips, thick thighs, short black hair, and dark swarthy skin, yet she's a pretty woman. She's wearing blue jeans and cowboy boots with my purple vest with no blouse underneath. Yes. I know I said that before. Tino is wearing a white shirt, starched, and tight Levi's. He's a big man, six foot two or so, weighs about 190 or 200 pounds. Every once in a while, they stop talking and kiss. I know why they've come over to visit me. They want a place to . . . you know.

Yvette asks, "Could we use the extra bedroom?"

I say "All right" even though I'm offended. I add, "I'm going to my room so I can get ready for work." My room is at the end of the trailer; I don't want to hear them. They're pretty wasted. I take my time getting dressed. I wasn't going back to the living room. I'd have to go down the hall and pass the spare bedroom to get to the living room, and I certainly didn't want to give Tino any ideas that I might be even remotely interested in him. I dislike a man who sweet-talks a woman into doing those things and who is constantly on the lookout for the next woman. That sums up Tino.

Finally, I heard Yvette holler, "Are you still getting dressed?"

Thank God, they've finished! I think as I walk down the hallway. Yvette is dressed and meets me in the hallway. "Think I'll get more beer from the refrigerator."

Tino calls, "Hey, Nadine, come in here for a moment."

Already, I'm on my guard. "I'm going to help Yvette get the beer," I say and go into the kitchen.

Yvette is surprised to see me. "Oh, go on back with Tino," she says. "I'll bring the beer back there."

Sounds planned to me, I say to myself. "It'll be more comfortable in the living room. Besides, we have to be at work at five," I say out loud. *Oh Jesus. They're putting the make on me!*

Yvette is spaced out, obviously. "Here" – she shoves the cold beer into my midriff – "take this to Tino. I'll be right there. I'm going to find something to eat."

"Yvette, you know I never keep anything in the fridge except for beer."

"Well, sometimes you have a loaf of bread and some baloney."

"If you can find anything, you're welcome to make yourself a sandwich," I say. I stay by her, holding the cold beer.

She says a little scornfully, "Are you afraid to take Tino the beer? Afraid he might make a pass at you?"

"No," I say. I go down the hallway. "I just don't like waiting on your boyfriend."

"Hey, he's not my boyfriend. I'm married, remember?" she throws back her head and laughs.

I stand in the hall. The bedroom door is ajar. Tino is buckling his belt. *Now why doesn't that surprise me?*

"Yvette said to give you this," I say and hold out the beer.

"Put it on the dresser, please," he says, still looking at the belt.

I'm not afraid, but I know that he will make a pass at me. I step into the room and place the bottle of beer on the dresser. He moves over to me. I go back to the doorway.

"Wait," he says and tries to reach for my hand. I move my hand out of the way quickly.

"Wait," he says again.

I stand in the doorway. "Yvette," I call.

"Be there in a minute," she says.

So this scenario is planned. Ugh!

"Nadine, I really think you're sexy," he says.

Christ! And he's just got through giving it to Yvette.

He lowers his voice, "Yvette doesn't reelly do too much for me. I mean, I like her, but it's you . . ."

Here he runs his small beady eyes over my body. *Is that supposed to turn me on?*

"Well, Yvette likes you a lot," I say and glare at him.

He lowers his voice. "But the only reason I'm with Yvette . . . well, it's you I reelly want to do it to."

And he looks right at my crotch. *Christ! I want to laugh. Reelly, I just reelly want to laugh.* But I don't. He'd take it for interest.

"I'm sure Yvette wouldn't like to hear you say that. Of course, I know you're only kidding. I know you and Yvette really like each other," I say lightly and try to save his face.

"No," he says stubbornly. "Yvette means nothing to me." And he licks his thick lips like he's licking grease off a taco. *Ugh!* I step out into the hallway.

"Well, that's too bad because she obviously likes you a lot. She's married, and she wouldn't be seeing you if she didn't like you a lot." I'm repeating myself. He thinks he sees an advantage.

"Come here," he says and steps back toward the bed.

I'd better straighten this out, I think.

"Oh no," I say and look Tino right in the eyes. "I like Yvette, and she's my friend (*obviously she wasn't for allowing this to occur*), but even if she weren't my friend, I . . . well, I'm not interested in you that way."

"Women like me. They reelly like me," he said.

"I'm sure they do," I said. "But it's not going to happen between us. Besides, I'm sort of Jason's girl."

"Jason doesn't like you," he said. "Not like me. Besides, his family would never let him marry you," he said.

"I don't particularly want to marry Jason either," I said.

"But me. Women like me."

God, he's repeating himself now.

"Hasn't Yvette told you about me?" he asked. Tino spread his legs and thrust his pelvis forward. I didn't look down. I kept my eyes on his eyes.

"What are you talking about?" I ask.

"I'm big," he said.

"Sure you are," I said. "I can see that. You're well over six feet tall . . ." And then I stopped and frowned. *Oh Christ!*

"Weel, you know what I mean. I have a big one," he said.

"Oh well," I say awkwardly and avert my eyes in embarrassment. *Uh-oh. Better look him in the eyes and get this straight.* "That really doesn't matter. I'm just not interested in doing that," I say firmly.

I walk out the door. He comes behind me, grabs my hand, and pulls me back into the room. He unbuckles his belt, unzips his Levi's, and pulls out the most enormous penis I've ever seen in my life.

"Look at it. Look at this." He grasps it with his hand and holds it toward me. "Women love it. They want it because it's so big," he said. "And I'm not even hard now. It gets bigger," he said. He looked with admiration at his penis.

I avoided looking at it. "I said I wasn't interested."

"You lie," he said. "You want it. No woman can resist it, and I make them feel good." He moved his huge penis with his hand. He lowered his voice. "I will make you cum better than any man can," he crooned.

He stepped toward me confidently, his thick lips wet with anticipation. I stood still. I looked him in the eyes and said clearly, "I don't want to sleep with you, Tino," and walked down the hall to the kitchen.

Yvette was sitting at the kitchen table. She didn't look all that happy. She seemed surprised to see me. *Did she really think that I would sleep with her boyfriend just because he had an enormous thang?*

I sat down across the table from Yvette. "I not sure why you waste your time with someone like Tino," I said. "Obviously, you really like him, Yvette."

"He's just so wonderful," she whispered and put her head down on the table. She ran her fingers through the short straight black hair in anguish. *Why, she really thought I'd hop into bed with Tino!*

I went over to Yvette, raised her face with my hands, and said, "I'm not attracted to your boyfriend, Yvette. I've never even liked him a whole lot."

Yvette looked relieved. She tried to focus her eyes. It wasn't just the drugs that made them cloudy like this now.

"I like him even less after today. I don't want to have sex with him, Yvette – not then, not now, not ever," I say.

And then she started to cry. It took almost thirty minutes before Tino and I could stop the crying. He said he was just testing her to see if she really loved him, that he liked me only as a friend. That he was testing me to see if I would be faithful to Jason and so forth. All crap.

Finally, we calmed her down. Yvette was reassured; even Tino was pleased to a degree. He'd managed to show off his massive manhood to me, and I . . . I just had this sick feeling I get in the pit of my stomach when people do the things they do.

I could have been Huck up in that cottonwood tree. Funny, too, about men. I don't tell my husband a lot about what happened in my past, but on the way to Austin, in a moment of sheer boredom, we start talking about unforgettable experiences. I tell him about Tino – not because I've seen him driving a school bus in Laredo, not because John Holmes actually had a Mexican twin in Laredo – but because people so easily misjudge others. What remains fixed in my mind today is not Tino's magnificent penis, but his incredulous astonishment that a woman, *after* having seen his magnificent penis, would actually refuse his sexual advances.

Now get this. My husband is the direct opposite of this Tino guy. He's intelligent, sensitive, educated, and the most manipulative person I've ever known. In the manhood department, he wouldn't be embarrassed to remove a loincloth, but he might hesitate if Tino were removing his loincloth too. But get this. When I'm telling Randall about Tino and I get to the part where Tino unzips his pants and belittles the star of *Boogie Nights*, Randall doesn't believe me when I say I didn't sleep with him.

"Now, Nadine, tell the truth. You fucked him didn't you?" And he looks across the seat at me, the same way Tino, all those years ago, looked across the hall at me.

TOGETHER AGAIN

She sat across the table from the boy. They sat in Dena's in Alice, Texas. The girl wore tight jeans, a nylon tank top, and clogs. At the most, she weighed eighty or ninety pounds. She was little, about five feet tall in her bare feet. She had light skin; dark, expressive little eyes; little breasts (it was obvious that she was wearing a push-up bra); and raven hair. She wasn't exactly pretty: her nose was too long, her chin was too small, and she wore too much eye makeup. She was maybe eighteen or nineteen. The boy was a little older. He was tall and squawky with deep-set green eyes. Freckles lurked beneath a golden tan, and brass glistened in the curly brown hair.

I watch them as I drink my iced tea. The boy furtively glances around the restaurant, his eyes jumping from one person to the next. He looks embarrassed and looks down at the table to avoid her eyes. The girl notices his embarrassment, and she looks casually, almost smoldering at the people. Her eyes travel from one table to the next, taking in the people. She sees no one she knows. The boy evidently sees no one he knows either and looks relieved. He covers up his embarrassment by asking, "You hungry?"

She nods her head at him. "A little," she says and then asks, "See anyone you know?"

"Nope," he says, acting a little bit surprised.

"Well, then I guess you're safe," she says with just a bit of an edge to her voice.

The boy flushes. "What are you talking about?"

There's a pretend quality to the voice that I don't miss. The girl doesn't miss it either. She shrugs her shoulders. "What are you going to have?" she asks as she turns around and looks for someone to wait on them.

The waitress comes over with the menus. The waitress isn't as eye-catching as the girl at the table. She's pretty plain Jane-ish, a cross somewhere between frumpy and natural. She has straight slightly dirty blondish-brown hair pulled back in a ponytail, golden skin like the boy's, and she's tall. The boy smiles shyly at the waitress; he's flirting with her very subtly, and the waitress smiles back.

Uh-oh. I stop reading *The Alice Times*. This is going to be better, no doubt. The girl with the black hair doesn't miss a thing. She glances at the boy and then at the waitress. She raises both thinly arched eyebrows a little, narrows her eyes, and watches the boy and then the waitress. *Uh-oh,* I say to myself again. The waitress blabs, "Welcome to Dena's." She doesn't look at the girl; she looks directly at the boy. I've seen her do this lots of times, fishing for a big tip. Smile at the man, ignore the woman, and you've got a substantial tip. "I'll leave these with you," she says, handing the boy and then the girl the menus. *Uh-oh.* The girl notices that the waitress hands the boy his menu first, not the other way around. The girl frowns. The eyes darken. She's quite an expressive thing. The waitress walks off. The boy and the girl look at the menus for a while.

"Made up your mind?" the boy asks in a low voice.

The girl answers, "I think I'm going to go with the hamburger steak."

The boy looks at the price, seems relieved, and says, "That sounds good. Think I'll have the same thing." They close the menus and look across the table at each other. They don't say much. The boy talks so softly, I can hardly hear him. He doesn't look the girl in the eyes either. The girl, on the other hand, isn't loud, but her voice is audible with a Southern tone. But it's not all Southern – it's tainted. The girl's got some Mexican in her for sure, with that black hair and those dark eyes. It's a pretty sure thing. The voice tells me she's spent more time with the white parent and little or almost no time with the Mexican one. I go back to reading the paper.

The waitress comes back. "Decided yet?" the waitress asks the boy. Again, she barely glances at the girl. "You aren't from around here, are you? You're not one of our regulars." And she smiles again at the boy. *Uh-oh.*

"No," the boy says, glancing up at her and quickly lowering his eyes. "We're from Bruni."

"Well, that's not too far from here," she said. They smile at each other again. "So what you gonna have?" she asks.

The dark-haired girl frowns again. She's a jealous one. Yep. Mexican blood for sure. She taps her nails in annoyance and quite deliberately on the table.

"We're both going to have the hamburger steak," the boy answered respectfully and softly. Jesus. That soft voice is so careful. I have to lean forward to hear what he's got to say.

"I'd like mine cooked well done," the girl says clearly.

The waitress turns around and looks down at her. "That's the only way hamburger steaks come," she says. She laughs a little and glances at the golden boy who laughs with her. The dark-haired girl doesn't laugh.

"I'll get your order right in," the waitress says to the boy. "What'll you have to drink?"

The boy said "tea," I think. The girl, I heard. She said coldly, clearly, "I'll have a Coke."

The boy glanced at the girl. The green eyes looked down his sharp nose at her. He turned his shoulder away from the girl with the raven hair and faced the blond waitress. "Thanks," he said and smiled again; he looked embarrassed to be with the girl. The waitress didn't miss this and glanced at the girl triumphantly before turning and walking off. The boy said something to the girl. She didn't answer. The head came up, proud; the eyes got darker.

The storm brewing, I thought and prepared myself for some unpleasant amusement.

The boy then turned back to her and talked softly, nicely to her. The girl wouldn't answer. She pretended to be interested in the people in the restaurant; she glanced at me once or twice. She knew I was watching, and the eyes narrowed and flashed angrily at me, so I went back to reading the paper.

The waitress came back with flatware rolled up tightly in a napkin. She placed one in front of the boy and walked off without giving the girl any flatware.

Uh-oh. Uh-oh.

The girl looked at the boy's flatware on the table, then she looked at the boy and waited. She said nothing. She waited to see what the boy would do. The boy said nothing. The waitress came back with the tea and the Coke. Still, the boy said nothing. The girl sipped her Coke slowly, but I saw the steel brace across her shoulders supporting broken wings. The boy can't help himself; he's flattered by the waitress's attention. He looks around for her, realizes the girl notices this, and quickly tries to cover his mistake by saying, "I thought I saw someone from Continental, but it wasn't."

"Thank God, it's not," the girl said resentfully. "We wouldn't want anyone from Bruni or Hebbronville seeing us together, would we?"

The boy pretends he doesn't know what she's talking about; he looks at her like she's a little touched. *What is it between these two?* I wonder. Obviously the boy and the waitress are attracted to each other. Rather, the boy is to the waitress, and maybe, on second thought, the waitress is attracted to the boy now. The boy's so polite, so respectful to the waitress. She's not used to that, and in front of her, the boy's condescending to the dark-haired girl, which flatters the waitress. The waitress brings the food over to the table and places the plates down in front of them.

"Enjoy your meal," she says lightly and flirtatiously.

The little half-breed's thin shoulders tremble. "And what do you suppose I should eat this with, my fingers?" she hisses. "Don't you think you should bring *me* some flatware also?"

She waves her hand contemptuously toward the boy's flatware. The boy stares coldly at the girl, looks at the waitress, and mutters, "I'm sorry."

"It's okay," the waitress says. "It's not your fault."

She turns to the girl who spits out at her in a clear, even voice, "It's *your* fault. You should have brought us both silverware."

The boy glares at the girl. The waitress says, "I'll get you some right away."

She gives the boy a sympathetic look. The boy is really embarrassed now. His eyes dart here and there in the restaurant. No one really pays too much attention; they're all hungry and shoveling food down pretty fast, some with both hands. The waitress brings the silverware and places it in front of the girl without saying a word and looks at the boy again in feigned sympathy.

Coconspirators. *Uh-oh. Uh-oh.* I turn to the sports page and read about the Alice Coyotes' recent loss.

"Thank you," the dark-haired girl says sarcastically. "It's so nice to *finally* get some service."

The waitress walks off. The boy chews his food with sharp jabbing bites. He's a handsome boy: clean-cut, all-American, mannerly. But his lips are too thin, too tight; the mouth, too small. Some of the food falls out of his mouth. He bends his head toward the plate and lets the bits of food fall out and onto his plate. The girl watches him pricking the hamburger meat; he's stabbing it, lifting the fork, tilting his head sideways to get the overly-large morsels into his mouth.

The girl is fuming. Her eyes snap and shoot infra rays at him – and at me too, for she knows I'm watching them. She cuts her hamburger steak deliberately, holding the knife and fork lightly, and brings the fork up smoothly and carefully to her mouth. She chews evenly; the boy chews jerkily. Both of them look pretty unhappy.

I sneak peeps at the girl from time to time. Her skin is so smooth; there's a faint flush to it now. She puts up a good front, but she doesn't fool me. The boy has humiliated her, and she, the boy, and the waitress all know it. And what's more, she knows I know it too. Her chin actually gets higher. She brings the food up dexterously to her mouth, and nothing – not an iota of a morsel – falls from the fork unto her plate. She dabs at her mouth with the paper napkin. Then our eyes meet, and for a moment, just for a moment, I think she might cry. But she narrows her eyes at me again, throws her hair back over her shoulders scornfully, and brings the chin up regally and straightens her shoulders.

The waitress comes back. "Would you like some dessert?" she asks the boy, ignoring the girl completely.

"Good god, no," interjects the girl. Then she adds flippantly, "Unless you have finger foods for dessert."

She rises from the chair, stretches, runs slender white fingers through her shiny hair, and walks out of the restaurant. The boy waits for the waitress to bring him the ticket. I get up and walk outside and get into my pickup truck. *Boy, she's all fire,* I think. *Tight hips, yet round and curvy.*

I start to drive off, but she doesn't notice me sitting there in my pickup truck, so I thought I'd hang around in case the boy doesn't come out. I really wish now I'd driven off, but I didn't. Somehow, I don't like to think about that girl. It is already getting dark, but I sit there and watch her. I was sure when the boy got out, she'd rake her nails across his face, but that's not what happened at all. She stood midway between the restaurant and the parking lot, hands dangling by her thighs.

The boy comes out of the restaurant, sharp and quick. "You didn't have to be so rude," he accuses.

She walks haughtily off. "*She's* the rude one. *She* didn't have to be so rude," she threw back at him.

The boy comes up behind her, cowboy boots stomping hard on the asphalt. He grabs the girl's arm; she shakes it off and walks quickly toward the car, swinging those tight shapely hips of hers, her black hair swaying side to side like a cobra. The boy comes up behind her again. Then his right leg shoots up quickly, calculatingly, angrily, like he is kicking a football for a field goal for an already lost game. The cowboy boot slams into the seam of those small hips. Hard. I hear the tailbone crunch. I see the girl crumble to the asphalt. The boy opens up the car and slides into the driver's seat. She lay there, crumbled, for a moment. I freeze. The boy stays behind the wheel: thin lips, venom-white eyes.

I am reaching for the door handle when she gets up. She stands, stunned, shaking for a long while. Again, I reach for the door handle, but then the girl touches her tailbone gingerly, takes a couple of steps hesitantly, and walks over to the passenger side of the car and slowly, carefully, wordlessly eases into the seat next to the boy. They don't look at each other. The boy reverses the Mustang, and they drive off; the boy, looking straight ahead, his wrist dangling casually over the steering wheel, his tires crunching the loose pebbles, flinging them on the asphalt.

My god, I thought. *What is it with those two?*

Lester pulls into the parking lot, slams the pickup truck's door, and asks me, "Hey, wasn't that Nadine Hernandez and her old boyfriend who just drove off?"

Nadine and the boy stayed at the Roadway Inn in Alice for a week. The boy went to work during the day. I didn't see Nadine anywhere, but somehow, I knew she was there. I drove around the Roadway Inn every chance I got for a few days, hoping I'd see her. Finally, I parked the pickup truck and went and peered through the window where the boy parked his red Mustang every evening. The curtains were open. Nadine was curled up on the bed by the footboard. There was something sacred about it, about that wisp of a girl on the bed all curled up on her side with legs drawn up. That sacredness spooked me. She saw me through the open curtain. She didn't move, and she didn't blink – just stared expressionless at me through the open drapes.

She and that boy had better leave each other. They're in for a mess of trouble. That pain she's feeling in her tailbone is nothing compared to what's gonna come later. God's just conditioning her. Then I stepped back, got into my pickup, and drove away.

JULIE IMOGENE

Her name was Julie Imogene Weatherly. She was my mother's only sister. Momma and Aunt Imogene grew up on Sugar Hill in Paris, Texas. They were inseparable during their childhood: two *cotton heads* (little girls with platinum-blond hair that was as white as cotton) fishing for crawfish at the pond and, later on, as young women, best friends sharing the same bed and whispering about their dreams.

When Momma met my father, when he was on leave during the Second World War, she fell head over heels in love with him (he was an exceedingly handsome man with a dashing smile with strong white teeth), and on the third day, they crossed the Red River and tied the knot in Hugo, Oklahoma. After the war, Daddy packed her things up in his brand-new secondhand convertible and took her south to Guerra, Texas, just thirty miles from the Rio Grande River. During the fifty-four years that my mother was married to my father, Mother went back to Paris only three times.

One of those three times was when Aunt Julie Imogene was in the hospital. Birdie Sherwood, who lived across the street from us in Bruni, came over and said Momma's father needed to talk to her on the phone.

After deliberating some – and without griping and shouting that he couldn't afford to take us to Paris and that he was sick and tired of hearing Momma asking him to take her to see her family – my father, two days later, said, "Get ready. We're going to Mr. Weatherly's."

We filled brown paper sacks with our clothes hastily, and Father drove us across Texas so Momma could see her only sister, Julie Imogene, before she died. Grandpa had told Momma on the phone that Aunt Julie Imogene "was all eaten up with cancer" and that the doctor said she had "about a week at the most."

She died the day before we got to Paris. My father drove straight across Texas without stopping, but Death was in a hurry and had given up hope: he couldn't wait forever for Avis Janelle to come back home and visit her family.

Three days later, after Julie Imogene Weatherly-Barns passed away, my Uncle Horace married the nurse who took care of Aunt Julie Imogene in the hospital while she "was eaten up with cancer." Grandpa, who shelved the family Bible on his lap and was revered for "not never ever saying a bad thing about anyone in his life," said dryly when he learned of the marriage, "Horace Barns did right well for hisself. Didn't waste no time grieving." Then, ashamed and with real wisdom – which I am, to this day, still in awe of – he added, "Our Julie Imogene wouldn't haf wonted him to be alone."

We didn't stay for the funeral; Father said he had to get back home. Had a job lined up, and jobs were scarce, and we drove south, straight back home without stopping. Even before we'd unpacked the car, Father was out the backdoor and walking down the alley to Maria Segovia's house – "that other woman's house" as my mother put it candidly and softly.

The neighbors said, "Gus did all he could. Took Janelle to see her sister. Just didn't get thar in time."

That was one of the three times Father took Momma back home to visit her family.

THE 1302 STUDENTS PRIOR TO READING "REPUBLICA AND GRAU" AND "CATHEDRAL" OR FERNANDO

They come into the classroom at Laredo University – some yawning, flapping in their flip-flops, squeaking in their Nikes, tapping in their stilettos – and Professor Hernandez gives them the assignment: "Free write about blindness." Many hesitate; again, Professor H has to remind them that free writing is just that – being free to write without rules.

"Write about blindness," she repeats. "Write about Ray Charles or Stevie Wonder, those blind men of song, or write about the blindness of fashion, if you want. Write about your friend who mixes polka dots with stripes and bizarre colors. Write about her pink hair, which might indicate that Lady Gaga and Pink are her best friends." And here Professor Hernandez laughs and then continues, "Write about the blindness of a friend or a person you know or know of. Write about the blindness of a time in your life." And then Professor Hernandez almost stops breathing. Her throat constricts, and Fernando – that blind teenage boy, like a neon sign over a dingy bar down San Bernardo in Laredo or down Bourdon Street in New Orleans – pierces her.

The cord to the neon sign is plugged in:

Fernando, the blind boy, lifts Nadine up and puts her on top of his shoulders. She is five years old. She hears in the blackness "Poor Fernando" and "Pobrecito" and "Pobrecito Fernando" for he is blind, and Momma and Daddy and Aunt Lucinda and Uncle Raul all say, "Poor Fernando" or "Pobrecito Fernando" and "Pobrecito Fernando" and "Poor Fernando," but it is Nadine, astride Fernando's shoulders, a blind boy's shoulders. And it is Nadine, astride Fernando, who is petrified, feeling Fernando's finger creeping ever so stealthily up and under her dress, working its way up and under the elastic of her panties . . .

And it is Professor H, in the bright glare of the classroom, who unplugs quickly and efficiently the neon sign and stands professionally in front of the class, balancing and blinding herself, pulling down green venetian blinds on that time in Bruni when the house was actually filled with her father's people and their friends.

Professor Hernandez prompts the students again in a clear, audible voice, "Write about blindness with open eyes," and then she shuts her eyes for just a moment. It is safe to do so, for the students are scribbling away on theme paper or tapping lightly on their iPads.

"I shut my eyes. I will not sink into the blackness," she whispers without sound to herself.

The students share their responses then discuss "Republica and Grau" and "Cathedral."

At the end of Professor Hernandez's Tuesday/Thursday class and when the last student echoes out the door, the neon sign winks, and Professor Hernandez sees the shadow of Fernando, an old man now, smiling disarmingly at pathetic tenderhearted idiots at an intersection (or is it in a cathedral?) as he lifts another little five-year-old girl upon his shoulders. Professor Hernandez bows her head, lifts the red pen high, and drips blood on a mountain of mostly worthless words.

STONES IN THE ATRIUM

Today again, she considered it. She couldn't make herself get out of bed. She tried feebly, pushing against the mattress with the hurt arm, to rise. She let herself fall back to the bed, for her feet were cold. She rolled out of bed, fetched a heating pad, climbed up the bed like a tree, and rested her feet on the heat. Still her feet were cold like her mother's blue-bloodied feet were on the day she died at LMC.

Oh hell, Nadine thought. *I'm not like my lovely gentle mother. I'm like Sherwood's mother's mother, staying in bed.* Ugh. It's six days . . . six days . . . what saves? On the seventh day, go to God? Thou shalt not kill. Thou shalt not commit adultery.

Take the Edna plunge? No! Think of the children. It is too cold . . . the thought of the cold, salty ocean . . . she couldn't . . . swimming out like that . . . seeing that crippled bird of failure dipping his wing into the sea . . . No, I don't think so . . . the Rio Grande River, maybe? Warmer, no doubt. The Red River? Redder, for sure. A warm bath, slit the wrists, let the red blood flow out? No. Ugh! All the red blood . . . what a mess for someone to clean. Sleeping pills? *Almost got to the finish line the time before at seventeen,* she thought. Ugh. That tube jammed in her nose . . . like the rape . . . Ah! That is the question. Was that a rape? That incident with that pudgy half-Mexican, half-French boy named Peter on Stewart Street in Laredo who cunningly pretended to be Colin's friend?

Funny. Her lover's middle name was Peter. Funny. In Edinburg, the red-haired, pock-faced professor's first name was Peter. That was back when she was twenty-three or twenty-four maybe. Funny . . . now *she* teaches American literature.

Odd it was that she could not get up to touch a book or a pen or a paintbrush or a hundred pounds of clay or a person. Odd it was that the desire to touch was gone.

Nadine shut her eyes. She saw Jesus stooping down at the foot of her bed, writing with his finger on the carpet. Through the French doors, with eyes wide shut, she saw that stones were piled high against the brick walls of the atrium.

The stones waited, then became impatient. "Pick us up!" they clamored. "Pick us up! Pick us up! Pick us up!" She fancied she saw Randall stacking more stones, heavier stones, bigger stones, in the atrium. No casting of stones from Randall, that was a surety, but it was she – Nadine Hernandez-Horchow – in the concrete garden, in a rage, who had lifted the massive sacks of soil when she was four months pregnant with Hamlet and flung them at Randall when he'd come home late that night after spending all day with that white-trash oilfield bimbo Guilda Jones. He'd shoved her, flung her against the patio wall, the cedar fence giving way, and she – and Hamlet too – fell like a split melon to the concrete floor. She felt the earth move under her feet. Wasn't that Randall's favorite song? The little band of gold, she remembered, made a little tinkling sound as it slid from her finger and rolled on the concrete floor. She remembered she had turned her head to the side, wondering what the sound was. It was a jingling and a tinkling of her wedding ring, and ever since then, it's been the sound of the clanging of bells, bells, bells.

She covered her head with the down comforter, ignoring Jesus at the foot of the bed and Randall in the atrium. With eyes wide shut, she saw Randall's left hand. No wedding band graced his hand ever.

MY WIFE'S COUSIN

My wife sickens me sometimes. She's wearing this Peter Nygard brown velvet pantsuit for the bank Christmas party, and she thinks she looks good. Maybe she does . . . a little.

I couldn't believe what her cousin looked like. I fell and fell hard. She came to school with Nadine and her sisters. Everyone stared. Here in Bruni, you don't see a lot of blondes, but Brittany (that was her name) had this fine silky blond hair cut short like a boy's. And to make things better, she had blue eyes. She was all white too, with the softest whitest skin imaginable. Nadine is a half Mexican – her father is Hispanic and her mother, white – from Paris in Texas. Brittany was Nadine's mother's niece.

I knew I had to see her again. Brittany sat with Carolina, Nadine's older sister, all during class. I couldn't take my eyes off her. All the boys were checking her out, but I had an ace up my sleeve: I was dating Nadine, so I could run over to Nadine's house after school and see Brittany again. Maybe she liked me. I think maybe she did.

During basketball practice, I played my hardest. There she was, sitting up in the stands, a pure white dove among a bunch of ravens. I shot from the side, swishing the net and making three-pointers left and right. I average about twenty-five to thirty points a game, so I think I impressed her. I raised my arm, caressing the ball with my fingers, and flicked it up to the skies; it surprised me when I missed. It hit the rim, and Bubba sprung up (he's a white Dennis Rodman), snatched it with a loud slapping sound, and brought it down, crouching over the ball, protecting it, long lanky elbows jutting out, and looking left, right, all around with a sneer. He spied an opening and threw the ball into a teammate's hand. They were down the opposite end of the court like a cyclone. They scored with a jeer. I glanced up at the bleachers. Brittany was watching Bubba now with interest.

In the locker room after practice, Bubba stripped off his shorts and headed straight for the showers. Like the Red Sea, the team parted almost in homage to Bubba. I wrapped my towel around my hips. Just last week, there was that conversation Nadine initiated about Bubba.

"I overheard Alma telling Dora that Bubba is huge." Nadine laughed. We'd had a lot to drink, almost a fifth of Jack Daniels among the four of us: Nadine, Nadine's younger sister Janis, her boyfriend Seth, and me.

Nadine and Janis looked at each other and shook their heads. "Naw, he couldn't. She's lying. Bubba? No way!"

Nadine glanced at me, boldly embarrassed. "Okay, Randall, you tell us . . . Well, is he . . . big or not?"

"Haven't noticed. Guess he's got a regular-sized one."

Seth erupted, "Ho, man! What do you mean a regular-sized one? What he's got between his legs is pretty impressive. Everyone knows that."

"I haven't. Naw. It's just ordinary," I tell Nadine and her sister.

Seth looked at me quizzically, attempted to stay silent, but then quipped, "Oh man, you just look next time we're all in the locker room." Seth always had to be right, never one to back down.

I laugh. "Ugh. Not me."

"Bubba . . . gosh . . . I never would have thought that. Bubba?" Nadine exclaimed.

Janis looked at her, and they both burst out giggling. "Naw."

When the bell rang, I ran into Nadine in the hallway between classes. "Hey, wanna go to a movie tonight?" I asked.

She smiled and lit up like a Christmas tree. "Yeah, that'll be fun."

"I thought maybe you wouldn't want to go since your cousin's here."

I was hoping she'd hesitate, but Nadine just tossed her long black hair over her shoulder and said, "Actually, I'd rather go out. I've visited enough."

"The movie is in Falfurrias. That means we'll have to leave around five in order to get there on time. Will that be a problem?"

I hoped I sounded considerate. I hoped that she'd rethink how long she'd be gone and say she wanted to stay home and visit with her cousin, and then I could suggest that she invite Brittany to come along, and it wouldn't seem like I was interested in her.

"No, it won't be a problem. See you at five," she said nonchalantly and went swinging her hips down the hallway.

Damn.

Mom was in the kitchen when I got home. I managed to talk Mom into letting me use her brand-new Town Car for the movie.

I went over to Nadine's house. She was in the living room with her cousin and sisters. Brittany lowered her eyes when I came in. She was wearing this short blue sleeveless dress, making her eyes bluer than AOL-icon blue. Her shoulders slumped slightly and her knees touched each other, yet the ankles were spread apart. I gulped. She giggled. I saw Nadine's eyes smolder. Boy, I'm going to have to play this real cool.

"Nadine, I came over to tell you that my Mustang wouldn't start (of course I lied), so we'll have to go in Mom's Town Car." I saw Brittany's eyes widen a little, so by now, she knows we're not poor like Nadine and her family are. Good. "I hope you don't mind."

"That's okay. It'll make the drive smoother."

"Well, it sure is a big car," I said. "And roomy," I added. Nadine didn't take the bait.

"What are y'all doing tonight? Just visiting?" I asked Carolina, trying not to glance at Brittany.

"Nothing? Absolutely nothing. Guess we'll stay here and talk," Carolina said.

"Hey, I just thought of something. Nadine, if you want to visit with your sisters and cousin, they can come along." Carolina and Brittany smiled. "The car's big enough for all of us and more," I said politely as Nadine looked down at the hardwood floor.

"Oh, we'd like to go, wouldn't we, Brittany?" Carolina said.

Brittany said demurely, "Yeah, it'd be nice. I've been wanting to see *Doctor Zhivago*. That is, if Nadine doesn't mind."

Nadine didn't say anything.

Carolina probed, "You don't mind, Nadine, do you?"

"Of course she doesn't mind," I said quickly. I really thought Nadine might say she *did* mind and then I'd miss the opportunity to be with Brittany.

"Well, Nadine?" Carolina persisted.

"No, I don't mind. It'll be fun." Nadine smiled at her sister and cousin and turned on her heel and walked out of the room without looking at me.

I knew I'd hurt Nadine's feelings. She has this frightening Miltonic Beelzebub pride, but I was too happy about reigning in Bruni, Texas, rather than standing meekly by and letting Brittany slip from my grasp. I was taking Brittany out. I was the guy from Bruni who was taking the blond cousin out. Of course, my girlfriend and her sisters were coming also, but like I said, I was too happy to care.

The evening wasn't all a disaster. Brittany took my breath away. She'd changed her dress. She was wearing a light yellow dress that was almost the same shade of her corn-silk hair. I'm not sure what Nadine was wearing. Probably some dress she'd ripped apart and remade. She could, everyone knew, take old secondhand dresses and faded shirts nobody else wanted and make some of the most unusual and eye-catching clothes. But don't ask me what she was wearing; all I cared about seeing was the blonde in the backseat in her corn-silk dress and corn-silk hair. On the way home, I kept turning around. I couldn't help it. I wanted to know about Nadine's cousin. I was mesmerized with the sound of her voice.

"Where are you from?" I asked.

"St. Louis," she answered.

"Have you always lived in St. Louis?"

She and Carolina glanced at each other and giggled.

"No, we just moved from Dallas."

I almost ran off the road turning around to look at her in the backseat. God, her legs were white and long! She had her knees kissing each other again and those ankles spread apart. I've never seen a woman since hold her legs like that. I know I'll remember her always like that, sitting in the backseat in my mom's luxurious Lincoln Town Car, giggling and answering softly and shyly, glancing at Carolina and then at Nadine, back at me, and then down at her knees. God, was she ever so sweet and innocent!

"Did you like the movie?" I asked her.

"Yes, it was a great movie." And then Carolina and Brittany laughed again as I ran off the road again for the umpteenth time.

"Maybe we can do this again tomorrow. Go to another movie," I said. And then I knew I'd made another mistake. No one answered. Nadine was staring straight ahead. Again, the car swerved.

"Maybe you'd better let me drive," Nadine suggested. "That way, you can talk to Carolina," she paused for just a fraction of a second, "and Brittany."

I pulled the car over and got in the passenger's seat. That way, I could turn to the side and see Brittany.

"Wait a minute!" Carolina shrieked. "Nadine doesn't know how to drive!"

Somehow it didn't matter. I was a little apprehensive, but all I could think of was the blonde with those big baby-blue eyes and those lovely long legs sitting in the backseat of my mom's car . . . and I wanted to be sitting next to that sweet, innocent, sexy girl-woman – not next to Nadine.

"Oh, there's nothing to it – driving, that is," I assured them. Nadine rammed her foot down, and the Lincoln shot through the night! She hit eighty in about five seconds!

I tried to continue talking to Brittany, but both Carolina and Brittany were screaming with fear and laughter. Nadine laughed scornfully, shrugged her shoulders, flipped her hair over her small shoulders, and said "That was kinda fun" when she slid into the passenger seat again.

Next day, I couldn't wait to take Brittany out again. I strolled over to where Nadine, her sisters, and Brittany were sitting with the pep squad and said hello.

Brittany smiled shyly and looked over across the gym at Bubba in his basketball shorts shooting baskets and practicing his rebounds. I was pretty happy; I'd been out with her last night, and everyone knew it.

And then I did something I don't like to remember. I asked again, pretending I hadn't asked the same question last night.

"Hey, Nadine. Want to go to another movie tonight?"

Nadine didn't answer.

"You can invite your cousin and sisters again." I couldn't help it. I *had* to ask.

No one said anything. It was pretty awkward for a time. Then I said, "We can get your cousin a date real easy."

Nadine looked relieved, and so did Carolina and Brittany.

"I guess so. It's okay with me," Brittany said and smiled sweetly.

I already had a backup plan. I'd ask Lars; he's no competition. He's short and pretty chubby, and he'd jump at the chance to date Nadine's cousin, and then I'd get to be with her again.

"Well, who should we ask?" I smiled and looked at Nadine then at Carolina and then at Brittany, letting my look linger on her just a moment longer than necessary.

Nadine shrugged and watched the team line up.

Carolina and Brittany whispered and giggled and whispered and giggled some more and then, after a while, Carolina said, "Brittany said she'd like you to ask Bubba if he'd want to go with us."

My hands felt heavy; I almost dropped the basketball I was holding.

I glanced at Brittany quickly; she was all flushed, the pink running up her neck into her cheeks. Her eyes involuntarily shifted to Bubba. Bubba leaped up, captured the ball, his elbows fended off any would-be attackers, and dribbled the ball across the court. Some of the players watched her out of the corner of their eyes, hoping that she might notice them, but not Bubba. He was into the game – focused, sweating, weaving in and out, and slam dunking the ball for a climactic two points.

"Sure," I said. "Sure, I'll ask him after practice."

You guessed right.

I didn't ask him, even though I knew Bubba would jump at the chance to date her.

I went over to Nadine's house after an hour or so and told them Bubba had a date and couldn't go, but that Lars could go instead. Nadine looked surprised, Carolina looked angry, and Brittany just looked crushed. Her face was all pink again, a different pink, but I didn't care too much. I'd have her again with me tonight, and she'd start to like me, especially after dating fat Lars.

But I missed the rebound. Brittany said she really didn't want to go and looked as if she was going to cry.

I croaked, "Well, then I guess it's just you and me, Nadine."

"It's just us then, Randall," Nadine said and looked through me.

Anyway, Brittany didn't come to school the next day with Carolina and Nadine. And in the late afternoon, Brittany and her family were gone.

Nadine walked over to the fence where Bubba was leaning.

"Hey, Bubba!"

"What?"

"I can't believe you'd turn down a date with my cousin. She's gorgeous and a real nice person," Nadine accused.

"Huh? What ya talking about?"

"Didn't you think she was pretty?"

"Yeah, I guess so."

"Then how come you told Randall you didn't want to go out with her last night?"

Bubba looked down at Nadine and said, "Randall never asked me to go out with her."

"That's not what Randall said," Nadine said flatly and walked away before Bubba could say anything more.

Bubba cornered me in the locker room after practice. "Hey man, how come you didn't tell me Nadine's cousin wanted to go out with me?"

I laughed. "Where'd you hear that?"

"From Nadine."

I laughed again. "You must have heard wrong, or Nadine was funning with you." And then I added, "Nadine's cousin has a boyfriend back in St. Louis."

"Well, I wouldn't have had time to fuck her, anyway. Maria wants it all the time." Bubba shrugged, swaggered naked over to the shower, and turned on the hot water.

So years later, Nadine and I are driving to Kingsville for the bank party. We're passing through Falfurrias, and I ask her, "Do you remember what movie we saw here when we were in high school?"

Of course, she won't remember; she never remembers where we see movies. I have a knack for it, remembering trivia like that.

"No," she says in a slightly bored voice.

"*Doctor Zhivago*," I say triumphantly.

"Hmmm," she says. "I didn't remember that. But I do remember the movie. It's one of my favorite movies," she adds conciliatorily.

"Do you remember who we saw it with?" I pursue.

"No. Who?"

"Your cousin, what was her name? And Carolina."

For a moment, Nadine doesn't answer. Then she answers, still in that slightly bored voice, "Yes, I remember that. You borrowed your mother's Town Car for that excursion. I wonder sometimes how you ever managed to talk her into letting you have it for that night."

We rode in silence for a while. Then Nadine said in real wonder, "My! I've never known a woman to be so obsessed with a man! She just couldn't stop talking about Bubba Matthews."

"Oh, Brittany didn't like Bubba," I insisted.

"Oh, but she did," Nadine said softly. "You should have heard her talking about Bubba."

We rode in silence for some time. Most of the time, I just nod or mutter "yeah" when Nadine talks. I really have lost quite a bit of my hearing in my right ear ever since I took that flight to Europe when I had the flu in my last year of college. There's not a lot of traffic on the Falfurrias highway this late at night. We rode in silence for several miles then, slicing the darkness, I hear Nadine say, "You know, I wonder sometimes about my mother. She was always so far away from her family. The Weatherly's only came to visit us two, maybe three times, once she married Daddy. I wonder if she would have been less lonely if Brittany had dated Bubba and then married him."

I winced.

I hope the darkness veiled my face. I still see my wife's cousin with the short blond hair, with her knees touching and her ankles spread, shaping the apex of her womanhood. I'm alone a lot during the day, driving down these South Texas highways and checking leases from Brooks County to Webb County. I liked Nadine's mother. When my brother was killed in that plane crash near Freer, Nadine's mother held out her arms to me, and she cried for me. She was alone a lot, I knew. People in Bruni weren't very nice to her, including my own mother.

The darkness hunched on our shoulders. Where the hell is the moon? We drive, my wife and I, in silence; and I know, as much as I'd like to deny it, that Nadine's mother would have been, as Nadine said, less lonely in Bruni if Brittany had married Bubba.

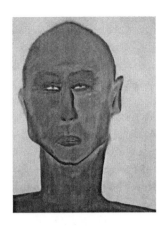

PRAYING TO THE HOLY GOD AND THE DEMON GOD

Naked, Nadine walked into the closet, closed the door, and pulled the lingerie drawer out to keep the door closed and to barricade outside forces. She carefully sank to her knees in the dark closet. She closed her eyes. She raised her arms high above her head, stretching fingertips penetrating the ceiling, searching for the Rulers. She lowered her arms slowly, ritualistically, to the eucalyptus carpet.

She visualized Dax with his thick phallus and visualized the passion he felt for her. He'd said once he knew he loved her for it was like a wave rushing over him. She reached high with her arms, wrapped her arms around Dax's neck, pulling him close to her. She whispered, chanted, "Dax, you love me. Dax, you desire me. Dax, it's Nadine you want, you love, you desire, you lust for. It's me you want. Dax and Nadine forever."

She repeatedly lowered her arms slowly to the floor and raised them heavenward. The wave rushed toward her stomach, pushing against her. She drew in her breath, feeling elation as she felt over the miles Dax's desire.

She prayed first to God. "God, make Dax love me. God, make Dax desire me. My Holy God, my demon god, don't let the Lust Life end." And then she prayed to Satan. Not even a shiver ran down her heart or spine. "Devil god. Devil god. Give me Dax's love. Make him desire only me. If he's fucking another woman, make him think of me only. Make Dax love me. Devil god. Holy God, do not forsake me. Hear my prayer, God. Dax and Nadine forever. Love. Lust. Life."

Again and again, she raised her arms and subsequently lowered her body to the floor. She repeated this for many minutes. Finally, she rose. She walked back to the bed, pulled the covers over her head, closed her eyes, and replayed moments with Dax. Once she told Dax, she pressed replay and relived their last time together. He'd smiled. "Boy, we've got it bad." Then she knew he did the same thing.

"Dax," she moaned and closed her eyes.

After her sleep, Nadine showered, letting the scalding water soothe her, and the blues bubbled from her soul. She was fearful that Dax would never come back. She turned the shower off, and then she heard the phone and the demon god wrote his number on caller ID. The Lust Life rushed through her, the blood sang in her veins once again, and the walk leaped into the age-old serpent dance.

She heard his "Hello." She jumped, she rocked, bowing to the gods above and below. "Dax, Dax, Dax, oh Dax! I'm so glad you called!" She didn't mask her feelings. "Oh, Dax, I'm so sorry I scratched you like that the last time and bloodied your back!"

And they were back together again, tearing at the LustLifeBlood, making Laredo livable.

THE DELIBERATE
BIPOLAR WOMAN

She waited for about twenty minutes. She wasn't sure she would call him.

He'd e-mailed her. "Can you get away for coffee about twelve thirty? Call me." She waited, not sure whether she wanted to even start it all up again; she hadn't seen him since August, and that was a disaster, so perhaps it was better not to even count that time. The time before that in May didn't go too well either. Now it was December. It's been eight months since she'd been with her lover.

You're bipolar, most likely. Impetuous, irrational. These are the symptoms that make one bipolar, she chastised herself. *I can just not answer like I've done many times before,* she thought; but instead, she wrote back, "The only real problem is where."

He responded instantly. "In a parking lot in your Excursion . . . I don't care." She knew that he needed her and wanted her. *Take it for what it is. You're married. You're older than him by sixteen years! Jesus! Take it for what it is, or just don't answer and stay in bed and stare at the wall,* she thought.

She reached for the phone and called him. "Can you come here?"

"Yes, but is it safe?"

"My son is home, but he's in the kitchen. I'll meet you at the door."

"OK. I'll be there in thirty minutes."

Well, how else will I survive? Better a quick rendezvous and something to remember rather than this staring at the wall and being so empty, she thought.

She went into the kitchen. "I'm going to the bank to deposit my checks. I'll be back in about thirty minutes. Will you be okay?"

Hamlet laughed. "I'll be fine. I have my laptop, and I need to check my e-mail."

"Okay, I'll be back soon."

The mother knew that what she was planning to do was morally and ethically wrong. Leaving her son unattended as she opened the door and allowed her ex-lover into her home was a wretched thing to do. Such quicksand she had avoided always! *Pretty unethical and sleazy and evil of me to do this, especially with my handicapped son in the other room,* she berated herself, but that didn't stop her.

She switched on all the lights to the Christmas trees: the one in the dining room, the two in the living room, the one in the study, and the one decorated with angels in the bedroom. She turned the two ceramic Christmas trees on in the bathroom. Everything looked beautiful for the nasty thing she would do. She walked hastily into the closet, put on black thongs and a black sequined pushup bra then pulled on a black lace crotchless bodysuit she'd worn for him before. She slipped on blue jeans and a button-down top over the crotchless lace bodysuit and slipped on black high heels.

She went out in the yard to wait for him. Just as soon as she stepped outside, she saw his blue Mini Cooper slowing down. In her driveway, there were six cars parked: a red Mercedes SL600, a brand-new silver Dodge Viper, an Excursion, a Range Rover, a lifted diesel pickup, and her son's handicapped van. She saw the Mini Cooper turn around and pull up to the mailbox.

What a little squattish car, she thought. She opened the Viper; she wanted him to see her new car. Once, when she'd just gotten the Range Rover, he'd acknowledged it with "I wish I could buy a new Range Rover." She'd ignored the comment. She retrieved some papers from the front seat and smiled up at him as he walked toward her. He said nothing about the Viper; he didn't even look at it. She said, in what she supposed was a friendly and businesslike manner as if she were talking to a supervisor, "Hi, I've got the papers ready for you now. Sorry I didn't get them to you earlier. I was swamped."

He took the papers from her. Amazing how quickly he got into the role. "That's okay. I understand."

"I have the others ready as well. Come in, and I'll get them for you. Again, I'm sorry I wasn't able to get them to you earlier."

The gardener watched them both and then turned back to blowing leaves off the driveway.

When she stepped inside the doorway, she raised her finger to her lips. "Hamlet is in the kitchen."

He glided in silently, nodding.

"Hamlet," she called from the hallway, "I'm leaving now."

"You mean you haven't left yet, Mom?" Hamlet asked and laughed from the kitchen.

"No. I fell asleep, but I'm leaving now." She closed the front door and bolted it. She took Dax by the hand and led the way. And then she had him in the bedroom. She closed the door ever so softly and turned to him.

She stood next to him. He was so tall – six feet three inches! She was only five feet tall. He'd lost even more hair. His hairline had receded dramatically since she'd seen him last. She felt sadness, but she rationalized that sadness and awkwardness beat boredom any day. Her life was so dull and boring. How she missed Dax in her life! She touched his chest. Then she pushed him deliberately into the massive cognac leather chair.

He spread his legs wide, and she knelt in front of him, her hands on his knees.

She must be quiet. Her son must not hear her, but somehow, she knew she'd get away with it. Who would suspect that she could be so callous and unfeeling – to fuck her lover (she wasn't sure she could call him a lover anymore) while her disabled son was in the other room, translating John from Greek to English? She'd kept the devil at bay for over eight months and then she just sort of shrugged her shoulders today and thought, *Anything is better than this living deadness*, and invited him over. Just like that.

He sat there, legs apart. She touched him lightly on the inside of his thigh. She wasn't going to change her mind; she knew that for a certainty, but he wasn't sure if she would or not.

"So what's the situation, really? Married? Living together? Baby on the way?"

He watched her. He didn't answer.

"I've heard all kinds of rumors. Am so curious. Married?"

He said, "No."

"Well, are you going to marry her?"

Again, he hesitated.

She laughed a little. "Living together?"

"We're spending more and more time together," he said evasively.

"Ah. You're living together," she said.

"We're spending more and more time together," he repeated.

"Baby on the way?" she asked again.

She pressed his inner thigh a little, moving her fingers upward toward his crotch.

"No," he said.

She smiled a little. "So are you going to marry her?"

"Probably," he said and watched her face closely. Then he added, "She gets along well with Regina."

She didn't answer for a moment.

"Want to change your mind?" he asked.

She looked away from him and around the bedroom. What would she do today to make her heart throb with life? She'd wait on her son, get her son something to drink and something to eat, take him to the toilet, lift him back into the wheelchair, get him his laptop, take him back to his room, turn on the TV, fetch a book or a blanket, perhaps have a conversation with her son, but most likely not. It'd be more of an evasive game there too. The son would want to go to a movie or go shopping or go out to eat, and she didn't feel like getting out and lifting him in and out of the Range Rover or driving the van. Yes, the son had brought the van home, but she didn't really want to do anything or go anywhere. There was just too much sadness and anger she felt when she took her son places. And people stared. People wondered why her son was like he was. And what was the real truth to that?

She looked back into the small brown eyes of her ex-lover, if you could even call him an ex-lover. Just a quick mutual fuck that lasted about thirty minutes or so and then silence for two or three weeks. This time, she hadn't let him fuck her for eight months. Did she expect him to remain faithful to her? To wait for her? She was married and had always known she would never leave her husband simply because to leave her husband meant to leave her children, and that was taboo. They were grown now: one was a true artist and talented musician working on a PhD in both art and music at UT in Austin and the other (the one with spina bifida and in a wheelchair) was a journalist for WSJ. She could leave now, she supposed, but Adele's "Think of the children. Think of the children" was the only real wisdom in that 1899 novel she taught in the 2328 class and perhaps the only real wisdom in life. They came home only during Christmas and holidays, yet divorce was never an option when they were children and even now when they were adults.

"No," she said and then asked quickly, "So what's her name?"

He didn't answer. She looked at him straight in the eyes. She shrugged her shoulder a bit.

"It'll be common knowledge soon enough," she said.

"Amelia," he said.

"Amelia what?"

"Amelia Sepulva," he said.

"Oh," she said.

"That's her married name. She was married to a real jerk that abused her," he said.

"Hmm, that's what most women say when they've been dumped," she responded matter-of-factly.

She didn't ask for the maiden name.

"Where did you meet her?" she asked, moving her fingers a little more.

"In a bar."

Her eyes widened a little, and she said nothing. But she couldn't resist asking after a moment of silence, "Where does she work?"

He didn't want to answer, but he did. "At the university."

"What does she do?"

This time, he wouldn't answer. "I don't know. She's a secretary or something." And that was all he was going to say.

So what now?

"How old is she?"

"Thirty-five," he said just as matter-of-factly as she'd been earlier.

"Oh," she said and glanced to the side and around the beautiful bedroom. He watched her face. She felt old, blanched.

"Deliberate cruelty is unforgivable." Tennessee's Blanche said that, but then, deliberate cruelty is necessary at times, she thought. She was twenty-one years older than his girl, live-in lover, and friend – the thirty-five-year-old dark Hispanic woman who was obviously all these things to him.

She listened; no sound came from the kitchen. Her son was e-mailing friends and thought she was gone. The house was always so cold and dark. The facts, as always, struck home. His new love was thirty-five; she was fifty-six. Hello! Do the math. He's no Ashton; you're no Demi. Slap yourself! The man would choose the younger woman, of course. It was one of those harsh-yet-necessary laws of nature. *Sounds like London,* she thought.

She thought, just for a moment, that he felt a little sorry for her. She didn't like that. She'd say something light and smart back to him, she thought, but she only repeated herself. "Oh," she said.

He sat in the chair, legs spread, with no bulge in his pants and no expression on his face.

And what now?

She pushed herself up. Once he'd called her bipolar. Even her sons had commented on the fact that she could be bipolar, and of course, Randall, at times, had called her mentally unbalanced – so she most likely was. Or maybe she simply was an unhappy, weak woman constantly searching for windmills. *I think I'd rather be slightly bipolar than unhappy,* she thought deliberately, trying to rationalize and excuse her wantonness and loneliness and her desperation. What were the symptoms of bipolar people? Impetuosity. Impulsiveness. Megalomania.

"I'd rather be bipolar than living dead," she thought and pulled her shirt up and over her head in one swift movement. He gasped. She took both hands and put them on the sequined padded black bra and pushed her breasts together. She took the lace bodysuit, which had slipped down, and raised it up and over the sequined bra. She smiled at him.

Looks like we're back at square one, she thought. She unzipped her Levi's and pulled them down over her legs and kicked them off. She put a black gossamer robe over the bodysuit and walked over to the bedroom door, testing to see if it was locked or not. It wasn't. She locked it and turned back to him. He still had not moved.

She knelt, almost in homage, and centered herself between his long legs again. She placed her hand on his belt and unbuckled it and unzipped his Dockers slowly.

She rubbed his underwear; she could feel his manhood with her hand. It stiffened and grew hard. She knew it wouldn't be like the last time, with him standing nude, hunched over in a corner of the room with one hand balancing himself against the wall and with the other hand jerking his limp penis, trying to get it hard again and attempting unsuccessfully to ejaculate.

Jee-Jee-Jesus! That was horrid! That was eight months ago – eight long agonizing months ago.

With both hands, she took the elastic band of his underwear and pulled them down, exposing his manhood. She gasped a little at the thickness and hardness of it. She looked at him, eyes a little playful, and bent her head down, letting her tongue, like a snake's, flick out of her mouth. She leaned closer and closer and then she pulled herself upward again slowly, eyes twinkling, as if she might change her mind.

He sat there impassively, as always. Perhaps that is what had attracted her to him: that impassive, unfeeling, untelling, unexplainable face of his. She pretended to rise and then she changed her mind, as if she really could not resist that marvelous thick part of him even though she had for eight long months. And sometimes, when she had weakened, he had resisted her and rejected her as well. Or when she had wanted him, he'd been fucking Amelia or planning to or preferring Amelia to her.

She felt her breasts again, pushing them up and down and apart and together as her tongue flicked in and out of her mouth. He tried to touch her breasts. Most of what he would touch would be the sequins and the foam rubber anyway, so she pushed his hands away, as always.

He waited with hands by his side. Her mouth opened wide like a snake's, unhinging her jaws, and then she lifted up on one knee and touched his lips with hers, and then they were kissing. His mouth was wide, and it covered hers with a fierceness and a sureness that thrilled her. He stuck his tongue deep into her mouth, and when it retracted, she thrust her tongue deep into his mouth. It was a dance, passionate and animalistic: his tongue in her mouth, her tongue in his mouth, and his mouth covering hers, her mouth covering his.

She stopped, looked him in the eyes, and moaned softly and pulled him deliberately by the shirt toward her and then she arched her back backward and fell on the plush green carpet of the bedroom floor. She spread her legs, moving the robe to her side and, with her fingers, pulled the black lace crotchless opening of the bodysuit apart. He saw the pinkness and wetness of her, and with his hand, he guided himself toward the small opening and then he shoved his hard thick beautiful manhood into the smallness and the wetness and the tightness of her.

She felt his manhood rubbing a little against the seams of the crotchless opening as he shoved it in and out of her, but it didn't matter. He was on top of her, fucking her again with his enormous thick beautiful manhood. Arching her neck backward, she looked at him. He was such a huge tall man! His mouth opened, and with a noiseless shout, his face twisted with animal lust. He lunged deeper into her, and she felt his juices erupt in her warmness.

Chests heaving, they stayed for a moment like that, the tall man on top of her. Dax was completely hers. And then she turned deliberately to the right side and reached for her jeans. She stood up, trembling and breathing hard, and pulled the jeans up and over the bodysuit. She took off the black robe and pulled a thin cotton shirt over her Victoria's Secret bra.

"I need a towel. Something to wipe with," he said and started to go into her bathroom.

"No," she said, almost curtly. "The window over the Jacuzzi. The gardener might see you."

And she picked up the black see-through robe and wiped his manhood once with it; even this was sensual between them. But she stepped away and put on her high heels.

He looked around the room as he wiped away her warmth and wetness. He pulled up his Dockers, which had fallen to his ankles, and zipped them with ease and finality. She was already unlocking the bedroom door. She listened at the opened door and then she stepped into the hallway. Her high heels echoed on the marble floors briefly, and then she remembered her son's presence and tiptoed across the hall. He glanced at the Christmas tree in the study and looked into the guest bathroom and glanced curiously around the living room.

"I'll walk you out," she whispered.

"No," he frowned. "Don't do that."

"You'll have to have some kind of papers with you so it'll look like you were picking up documents or something," she said logically.

She took some paper from the printer on her desk in the living room and handed the sheets to him. He rolled them up in one hand as she opened the door, and he walked out into the daylight and was gone. Just like that. After all that heaving on the floor, all thirty minutes of that, she was standing at an open door, watching her ex-lover (if you could call him that) who had left his wife and his little girl, not for her, but for another woman – this Amelia something or the other who might or might not be pregnant with his child and who was ugly and very ethnic looking and who was living with him and who would be his wife soon, or was already, and who was thirty-five.

Already, Dax had gotten into his Mini Cooper, and she stood and watched him turning the corner. She watched the construction workers busily remodeling the house across the street, making an old house new again, and watched Pablo, the gardener, tilling the dirt under the mature oak trees in the front yard. Her eyes traveled over all the vehicles in the driveway, finally settling on the brand-new sleek silver Viper that her husband had bought her for her birthday.

"What a wonderful husband you have, Nadine," all her colleagues had said enviously when they'd seen the new car.

"Ahhh! Oooh! I adore him. I absolutely adore him! Makes turning fifty-six less painful," she'd responded with a little laugh. But now, in the clear sunlight, her heart hardened like "The Rocking Horse Winner's" mother's heart, and she enunciated deliberately, "Baby killer, baby crippler," and almost struck the Viper.

Her son called from the kitchen, "Mom, are you home?"

"Yes, it didn't take too long. Got the checks deposited in the bank. I was afraid if I didn't deposit them, they'd be voided." The mother closed the door and went into the kitchen. "Want me to fix us a cup of hot cocoa?" she asked cheerfully as she put a dented saucepan, which wobbled ever so slightly, on the back burner.

For a week, Nadine blocked the ugliness from her mind, or pressed replay and relived the wantonness of kissing Dax again, or worked in the yard tilling the soil and uprooting weeds, or washed all the dust-covered vehicles in the driveway, or graded D papers. At midnight, she dusted the bookshelves, rearranged books pushing *Anna Karenina* and *Madame Bovary* to the back, stacked her grandfather's Bible in clear sight on the coffee table, painted a picture of a naked woman spread-eagle with a rosary draped between her legs, cut crosses between the inside of her thighs, and finally crashed. She lowered the blinds, turned the air conditioner down to sixty degrees, and slid between the sheets; she was burning hot and stared at the ceiling. Sleep did not come and would not come. Nadine wryly whispered in the darkened bedroom, "Macbeth doth murder sleep."

ON READING DOSTOEVSKY'S "BOBOK"

Nadine sat upon a man's tombstone and "Bobok, Bobok, Bobok," whispered, chanted, screamed from the dank earth. "Ahh," she sighed and recited softly, "an imperceptible spark of life is still glimmering." The page flashed and stuck, page 261.

The spark of life has dimmed . . . gone out . . . where's a match? Heh, heh, heh! "The moral stench." She saw the words on a page, and the page flashed as a camera flashed in her mind, page 262. "The moral stench" permeates all.

How can one not be ashamed? Nadine thought. She cringed. "Tell me your stories," the whisper rose from beneath the stone.

"Tell me your stories," the whisper again rose from the dank earth. The night wind rustled the plastic flowers placed on the graves around her. The night air chained her. One lone car drove down Saunders in the hot night. The man drove straight ahead, looking neither to the right at the city cemetery nor to the left at Laredo Medical Center, which had replaced the now abandoned and vandalized Mercy Hospital where she was born.

"Tell me your stories. Tell me your stories. Tell me your stories. Tell me your stories." The whisper became a chant. Voices joined, "Tell me your stories."

"Tell me your stories!" The scream sprung from the earth. Little anthills of soil ruptured and spread around the tombstone.

Nadine sat with legs crossed on the man's tombstone. She raised both arms high to the moon. The moon took a white cotton washcloth, the kind her mother had placed on her face as a child when she was feverish, and wiped the dirt clean from her uplifted face. Amidst the whispers, chants, and screams, Nadine kept her face lifted up to the moon. No shiver slithered up and down her spine. The moon bathed her.

"Achoo!"

Nadine knew not where the sneeze had come, but only then did she uncross her legs, lightly jump to the ground, and carefully climb the hurricane fence to access the street. No cars were coming. She carried in her backpack her stories, all tightly wadded up and trailing along. Tied to the backpack with sisal rope were the stories, all neatly bound, of the man upon whose tombstone she'd rested.

She walked down McPherson, climbed into the white Range Rover, and headed across town to Regency.

She unlocked the huge white door silently; she could hear her husband snoring from the master bedroom. For some unexplainable reason, Shakespeare's three bitch witches and their "Fair is foul and foul is fair" came to mind.

"NOW, NOW, CRISSY . . ."

"Now, now, Crissy. You know I love you more than your mom, but you know how it is. I can't tell your mom. If we did that, told her about us, it would break her heart. And she's not in the best of health. She could have a heart attack and die. She's overweight as it is. That's why we're here at Bonanza's Bar-B-Que. She's on that Aileens' diet, wants to eat just meat. She's trying to lose weight so I'll be interested in her again, but I don't love her, Crissy. It's you I love."

He tells me this – whispers it, really. I am sitting at the end of the picnic table at Bonanza's in Bastrop, Texas. I put my head on the table. It's an awful thing that I am doing to my mother. I don't know what to do. My mother doesn't want Danny to be unhappy. She is so afraid he will leave us. We are afraid too. I hope no one knows what I'm doing. I see them all sitting on the other end of the table. They are too far away to hear us, but just in case, Dad . . . (I have to call Danny *dad*. Both my mother and Danny insist I call him that. My real dad's name is Steve. He does drugs, and he and my mom hate each other.) Anyway, Dad is careful not to let anyone let on.

He tells me, "Tell them you don't want barbecue. Please, Crissy, tell them that. I need you, Crissy. Your mom is older and fat now. I just can't do that to her. I can't put my . . . you know . . . my, well, you know . . . I can't put it in her. You're the only one it wants. I've never put it in anyone I don't care about. I know I should love your mother, and I know you love her, and I should too, but the only reason I stay with her is to be around you. Please, Crissy."

"Please. Just tell them that . . . that you want fried chicken, and we can use that as an excuse and leave, and then we can at least touch each other in the car. Won't you let me . . . just touch it. Crissy, if you let me just touch it with my hand . . . just a little bit. That's all I'll ask . . . all I'll ever ask of you."

I look down the end of the table. My Aunt Nadine is watching us. I put my head down on the table again. I don't look up. I hope she doesn't know. My mother is, of course, blab-blabbing real loud to everyone about how she's on a diet and how whoever goes on this diet will lose tons of weight. Well, if she wouldn't have gotten so fat, maybe Dad (not my real one) wouldn't be sitting next to me, making me ashamed.

Danny takes my hand. I say, "They'll see you."

He says, "I don't care. Let them see me."

I pull my hand away and cry.

My Aunt Nadine asks me from across the table, "Are you okay, Crissy?"

My mom looks at me quickly. "Oh, she's just sulking. She didn't want to come with us. She's pouting. She wanted to stay in Pampa. She wanted to stay with her friends. Don't mind her," my stupid mom says.

Aunt Nadine says with a smile, "I can't imagine that."

She says this with just a smidgen of irony, just a tad too polite, and she looks over at us again, inquisitively. I can't help it. I just can't look at her.

"Are you sure, Crissy, that you're all right?"

I don't look up. What can I say, anyway? That Dad (God! I hate calling him *dad*!) is pressing his leg against mine? Ha! Danny tells me softly, I'm not sure if it's a threat or not, "You better look up and say something to her. If anyone knows about this, they'll blame us – you too – and then I'll have to leave, and you know what that'll be like. Your mom won't have no money again."

I shake my head no. I don't look up at Aunt Nadine.

Finally, Danny says, "Oh, she's okay, Nadine. Just doesn't want to have brisket. Wants chicken instead."

"Look up, Crissy. Please, please," he says ever so softly to me.

My mom says, "Oh, she's okay, Nadine. Let Danny talk to her. He's really good with the kids. You know he has three daughters of his own, and he treats Crissy as good as his daughters. Better than his real daughters. He's a fabulous father."

My great-grandfather looks at her. "Yep, he's a good man, Gabby! He has to be to put up with you!" And everyone laughs. They all get in line to order their meat and sides. Pigs!

Danny presses his leg a little closer to mine. I've never had no boy, never no man, press his leg against mine like Danny is doing now. I am afraid, but (I know this sounds weird) it *is* a little exciting in a way, I guess. I know it's wrong. Danny is my mom's husband, but Danny would really rather have me than my mother. He says so all the time, even in the middle of the night. When my mom is tired, it's Danny in the middle of the night who gets up to see if I'm okay.

He says she's always tired and that she never satisfies him. That she's old (she's thirty-six now) and that she's so overweight that he can't even think about it. He says I'm pretty and so young and a woman. I don't even have breasts. My mother has these big breasts – but then she's pretty heavy, so naturally, she'd have big breasts – but he says he's not turned on by her cowbags.

He pleads, "Please, I just need to be alone with you instead of all these people."

I know too what that means. I hate being with all my relatives 'cause I feel so stupid all the time, and there they all are, talking with my cousin who's twenty-one already, and just 'cause he's in a wheelchair, everyone is trying to act as if he's so smart. He is, I guess. But everyone is trying to act like Hamlet's not in a wheelchair or that it doesn't matter if he's in a wheelchair or not – when everybody knows it really *does* matter.

Maybe we could leave. I lift my head up and look around. Everyone is coming back to the table with their plates loaded with barbecue and sausage. It smells good, but Danny says, "Crissy is a little sick to her stomach. I think I'll take her down the road to Kentucky Fried Chicken and get her something else. Chicken might be easier on her stomach."

He gets up and takes me by the hand and puts his arm around me. I don't look up.

"Danny is just so good to the kids," my mom says again.

Sometimes I just want to vomit on her! She's said that for the umpteenth time tonight! Everybody is nodding their heads and shoving food in their mouths and saying how great a dad Danny is. Like, yeah, I guess so. My real dad was a jerk – or so my mother says. I wonder about that 'cause we never see him no more.

My friend Sam (Samantha's her full name) told me my real dad ran off with my mom's best friend – maybe that's just gossip, but I bet not. Anyhoo, Sam's always spending the night with me and always tickling me in places she shouldn't. Dad – Danny, that is, not my real dad – doesn't like her. He's pretty pissed when she hangs out with me. I don't know which is worse, Dad always touching me or Sam. No, Dad's worse. At least, Sam isn't my mother's husband or someone's father.

Aunt Nadine is wedged between my Uncle Randall and their son in the wheelchair. The other son, Brandon, stands politely and closely by their sides, almost as if he's on call.

"Maybe someone should go with you," my Aunt Nadine says. She's pretty insistent. No one pays attention to her. Like I said, they're all chomping down on their sausages. Anyway, no one likes her at all. When my Uncle Randall, he's my blood uncle, went away to college, Aunt Nadine went nuts they said and ended up living with some old man that rode about on a Harley. Then she came back, and they snuck off one day and got married before my great-grandmother or anyone else could stop them. My other uncle, Uncle Sylvester, who's from here, and who lays around all day long smoking weed (how cool is that?), once shouted out after drinking too much, "Hey, Nadine! Everyone's always wondered why Randy married you!"

Aunt Nadine, with eyes flashing, came back with, "You're a jackass, Sly." Ho. Boy.

Nadine said again, "Someone ought to go. She could stay here, and you could go get the food for her."

"No," Danny says quickly, "you all stay and eat." He glances around at everyone with little weasel eyes. "The fresh air might be good for Crissy. It's pretty smoky in here. I'll take her. I don't mind. Besides, I haven't ordered yet." He takes my hand and pulls me up from the chair, and we go out the door.

I don't look at my mom, but I hear her telling everyone how she can have as much meat, lean meat, as she wants, and then she'll lose the weight she's put on. Her plate is heaped high with brisket. She looks like a halfback for the Cowboys.

We get in the car. I'm scared to death, but I'd rather go than stay with all those losers who are related to me and who pretend they know everything but really don't.

We drive without saying anything for a while. Danny passes by Kentucky Fried Chicken. I start to cry out, "Hey, ya missed it!" because I am hungry, odd as that may sound, but somehow, duct tape covers my mouth and I'm unable to utter any sound at all. I want to say "Turn this car around, you idiot! You old leech!" but I remain silent. I don't want Dad to leave my mother or Derrick, my brother. Maybe if I let him kiss me a little, then he'll think I'll give him something more and then he'll stay. But I won't let him do anything more. I'll pretend I like it a little bit, and then we'll go get the chicken and go back to Bonanza's Bar-B-Que.

Dad parks the car down some dark street (Wilson or Chestnut or Chesthill – who knows?) and says, "Boy! Am I glad to be away from that crowd! Actually, you're the only one I really like and feel comfortable with." In a way, I'm glad to be away from them too. They always want me to push Hamlet around in his wheelchair, and everyone says how good I am to be so good to Hamlet. But I know that they just don't want to have to push him around themselves; it sort of gets old doing that, you know, pushing someone around in a wheelchair.

I feel his hand on my jeans. "You're the only one, Crissy, who's smart enough to understand what a man feels."

That scares me, but it kinda makes me feel more grown up than ever. He places his right hand nonchalantly on my thigh. I don't say anything. Man, is it hot! And sweaty! And his hand trembles ever so much. I almost want to laugh. A giggle bubbles up from my throat. I think that encourages him.

But the thing is, I've never had a man put his hand on my thigh before like I said. Anyway, it's not all bad – except that Danny is my dad . . . well, not my real dad.

He spreads his fingers ever so slightly, his pinkie spreading outward, curling upward slightly, touching almost my crotch, and then I get this real uncomfortable feeling in the pit of my stomach. My jeans get a little moist, and this smell rises up to my nostrils, and I am embarrassed. How come that smell comes from my jeans? I hope Dad doesn't smell it, but he does!

He whispers huskily and real deep like a dog growling but kinda gentle too. "I know you like what I'm doing, Crissy girl, because I can smell your scent. It's the sweetest smell. Not many women have that nice smell. A lot of them just plain stink, but you, my god, you smell so . . . so . . . so . . . You're the only one I know who smells so . . . kinda animal like . . . and so much like a woman."

I don't know what's happening to me. I really think he is a dork . . . a geek. But he's my dad – I mean, my stepdad. He whispers, "Please just let me touch it. That's all I ask. Please, just let me touch it once."

I'm too scared to do anything. It's like I'm paralyzed or something.

He continues softly, persistently, running on breathlessly, "It would mean so much to me, Crissy. You know I wouldn't ask you to let me if I didn't love you. I care about you, Crissy. I'm in agony, you know, thinking about you, dreaming about you. Just look down for a moment at my pants. See how that bulge is there? I can't go back with it like that. What would they say?"

I panic. What would they say? They'd blame me, I'm sure. Mom is always blaming me for everything! She'd say it was my fault! His pinkie reaches almost to the center of my jeans. It feels kinda good, and I don't really want him to stop. I've never had a boy want anything to do with me like Danny does, and Danny's a man, not a boy.

I say kinda shy and offhandedly, "Okay, but just this once." That's all I'll let him do and then he'll stop, and he'll be satisfied. And then we can get some chicken (I am pretty hungry) and go back to Bonanza's, and no one will know any differently.

And he reaches out ever so slowly and ever so surely and touches me . . . right there . . . in the center of my jeans. I didn't realize it was wet until he said, in awe and with a little bit of pride in his voice, "Why, Crissy, it's wet!"

Yeah. Right. Like I've done something really good.

"That means you like it . . . kinda? That means you are a grown-up woman. You like it, me touching you down there. Don't you? Crissy girl. Girl woman, say you like it a little. Just to please me. Just to please your dad," he adds, just in case I've forgotten that he might leave my mom who's blown up like the Goodyear blimp.

Now why did she have to get fat? But then, she wasn't fat when Danny first married her. Even way back then, he'd insist on bathing Derrick and me "'cause our mother works all day and is tired, and that's what dads do if they really love their kids." I'd glare at him and make the soap bubbles rise like white mountains to cover up my body, but Danny always managed to make a game out of bathing, and he'd blow the soap bubbles away or scoop them with his hand piling the bubbles up high on my head to make me look like the Queen of Sheba or his ivory snow queen. It wasn't until later that I found out about Marilyn Chambers and her commercial being pulled from prime-time TV because she opened a green door.

"Crissy, would you let me kiss you on your lips? I know it sounds strange to you, but men really like to kiss a woman's lips. Means they really, really like the woman they're with. Would you? Maybe just on the cheek here," he says and leans over and places his lips on my cheek. "Oh, Crissy," he moans ever so softly, and again it comes out like a gentle growl, and he moves his hand just a little on my thigh, bringing it up again to the center of my jeans. And then he brings his face down to mine, and he puts his lips on mine. It's my first kiss – first real kiss. It's not a Dad-kiss. Danny's not my real dad.

"I've never kissed anyone like that, Crissy. Never. I'll never kiss anyone like that again. Only you. I could never kiss anyone again after you. May I kiss you just once more?" he whispers, his voice catching.

"You can't tell anyone," he says. "We can't ever tell anyone. They'd make me leave your mother. That's not so bad, but they'd make me leave you, and I just couldn't live anymore. Let me, let me, let me just kiss you one more time," he pleads.

I look down at his pants, and I see his bulge. And it thrills me a little that I could have such power over a man like Danny to make his pants grow so tightly around him. And then he brings his face closer to mine and I kinda sink down in the car, and then Danny is kissing me again. He reaches up and pulls my chin down just a little bit, and my lips open, and then his tongue is in my mouth.

THE LOBSTER WOMAN

She went into the art building quickly. Douglas was sitting in his office. "Hey, Douglas," she said as she went past.

She went straight to the clay bin and took out several handfuls. It had a smooth, just-right wetness to it. She slammed the hunks of clay on the table then scooped it up and found an unoccupied space at one of the tables. She asked Jesus, "Is someone working here?"

"No," he said.

"Mind if I work here?" she asked.

"Go ahead," he said.

"I like what you're doing." She placed the clay on the table and moved over toward him. She touched lightly, appreciatively, with her fingertips the coiled clay vase he had sculpted. "I like the coils, the variety of sizes, the shapes," she said. She squatted down to see the piece at eye level. "I also like the open spaces. It gives the vase a delicateness. The grapes scored onto the coils make it even more delicate." She touched the vase at different points, ran her fingers around it. "It's a beautiful piece," she said, looking at him straight in the eyes.

The young man seemed pleased.

Then Nadine, with her red hair glowing copper in the sun, went into a trance almost. She blocked everyone out. She ran her fingers over the clay, slammed it and wedged it, rolled it into coils, shaped it into wedges: small, oblong, fat, thick. Every once in a while, she dipped her fingers in a large Tupperware bowl, then she wiped off the excess clay on her jeans or her T-shirt at times. She pushed the long unruly hair to the side, leaving bits of clay in her hair. It didn't matter to her, this clay, whether it got in her hair or on her jeans, for she was lost in the whirlpool of obsession. She slammed the clay on the table, piling up the wedges and the coils in about a twelve-inch-by-sixteen-inch area.

"You aren't going to use a board to put it on?" Jesus asked.

"Nope. If I like it, I'll wire it off and slide it onto a board," she answered.

She began smoothing the clay, forming a face. She pounded the clay into shape: a broad forehead, small eyes, and long high cheekbones. She sculpted a mouth that pursed somewhat; she changed the mouth several times. First it was wide and open, screaming in anguish, and finally, it was simply parted in a slit. She took away even more clay from the eyes with the looped wire tool, flicking the clay to the side, wiping excess clay on her jeans. The lids of the eyes, half-closed over tiny eyes, looked hollow and unfulfilled, and the cheekbones were molded higher up. The mouth was pouting, slightly opened, turned downward to a point.

Unhappiness, discontent, yet beauty triumphed somehow in this piece. The nose she elongated, placing a small hump in the bone in the middle of the nose. She took the wire tool and scooped clay from the nostrils and, with a skewer, pierced the nostril straight through until she hit the table. The music from the radio danced in her blood, in the tools, in her fingers, and even her hips moved in time to the beat. The sunlight streamed in through the old Fort McIntosh Building's windows, and the shadow of God was somewhere lurking near, emerging from her fingertips. This face on the table knew how it was to fall between missing boards to the murky shallow water below, to feel pain, to battle lust, to control lust, and then through controlling, to lose in the end.

"The face is much too two-dimensional," Nadine muttered to herself and stepped back to survey the piece, then she looked around the room. Students were forming rain sticks, placing slabs of clay over tubes and cylinders. She spied a cylinder about ten inches in diameter. She covered it with newspaper, took her wire tool, and holding the wire tightly with both hands, sliced the face away from the table, lifting the face with one swift sure movement and slapping it onto the cylinder. She molded the clay around the cylinder, clawing bits and pieces of clay to glue it into place, then she pinched coils, bits, wedges, and thin slabs of clay around the cylinder to form the hair.

The woman's face was now three-dimensional, complex.

Douglas came up to her. He stood close to her as she smoothed the cheekbones and smoothed the delicate chin. "Did you read in the paper about the woman? About the lobster woman?" he asked. His eyes were dripping semen.

"No, I've only been reading the *Norton Anthology*. We're on Sherwood Anderson and his grotesques," she said. "I keep reading his other stories that aren't in the anthology. I read one story by Sherwood Anderson, and it seems like I have to read as many stories by him as I can get my hands on."

Douglas shrugged. "Yeah, yeah," he answered. "But this woman and the lobsters, didn't you hear about it?"

"No. I go for days without turning on the television or the radio," she explained.

"Well, it seems this woman would get in the bathtub with these lobsters . . ." Douglas's voice got husky, low.

Nadine burst out laughing. "Oh no! Oh god, no. You're making this up," she accused him and laughed in his eyes.

She kept on with her fingers now touching the lips, shaping them, perfecting them into sensual lovely lips. Douglas moved closer to her while Jesus stared quizzically at them both.

Here goes Douglas with another dirty story, she thought.

"No, really, it's true. Jose is going to bring me the newspaper article in a moment," Douglas said. "It seems like when she got horny, she would take a bath and put these lobsters in the tub with her –"

Nadine interrupted, "I don't believe it. You're joking."

"No. Really," Douglas said, "I'm not. She'd get in the tub, and the lobsters would fan their tails up and down in the water, and this would excite her –"

Again, Nadine interrupted. "Oh no. No woman would. You can always find a man for that sort of thing. Someone made that up," she protested.

But Douglas was really getting into the story now. "Well, she put her lobsters in with her this last time, and one of them happened to be a female lobster that was pregnant, so she backed up and deposited her eggs . . . well, you can guess where. Naturally, in the warmest place ever," he said.

By this time, Nadine's hands had stopped moving. *The piece, the clay, mustn't be tainted*, she thought. She removed her hands from the face, placed her hands in the Tupperware bowl, and rubbed the clay from her hands, wiping her hands slowly on her jeans, mouth agape, staring at Douglas. *How could any man be so crude? What kind of man does it take to tell such a story?* Still, she didn't discourage it; it was somehow like trying to figure out the Mapplethorpe self-portrait with the bullwhip coming out Mapplethorpe's hairy, and certainly ugly, rectum.

Douglas continued, "Anyway, a week or so later, she starts getting these awful cramps. So she goes to the emergency room, and there they find out the lobster eggs were growing in her womb."

Nadine laughed out loud in sheer disbelief and in sheer astonishment, but mostly at Douglas. (What was it his wife called him? Grizzly.) *He probably has an erection by now*, Nadine thought.

"Oh my god," she muttered, barely audible. Then, "You're pulling my leg, Douglas. I don't believe it," she said steadily.

"No. Really," he said. "Can you imagine a woman being that horny?" he asked.

Nadine said, "No, no, I can't," and placed her arms across her breasts and stared at Douglas.

The phone rang, and he reluctantly turned to answer it. The students went back to work. Everyone avoided each other's eyes.

No, I can't imagine, thought Nadine to herself, *how a man can tell such a story. Any woman would be afraid to touch a man who told such a beastly story – grimly, grizzly, grotesque. Wonder what Sherwood Anderson would have done with such a story? Such an anti-heroine was more grotesque than Alice Hindman.*

She took her hands, baptized them with the clay water, and went back to molding the eyes. The eyes became sadder, more pained, more shrunken into themselves.

Men. Bah! For a moment, she thought she might vomit. She pinched little balls of clay between her index fingers and thumbs and stuck these into the earlobes of her clay woman.

THE PROUD MARRIAGE

He curled up his fingers and made his hands into fists, which never flinched.

"I've never liked you," he spat.

His words were Carl Sandburg's "hard boots."

You can't take those words back, Nadine thought as she narrowed her eyes at her husband of thirty-seven years.

He walked off proud; she stayed rooted to the floor and never said a word.

AHHH, MARIA!

Professor Hernandez is looking at the picture her student hands her. It is a picture of Josie's great-grandmother, Maria Segovia. Professor Hernandez holds the picture lightly between fingertips; she is composed.

She smiles at the student. The student has driven from Jim Hogg County to attend Professor H's 1301 class. The assignment was basic: bring a photograph to class and write a descriptive essay. The student has chosen a picture of her great-grandmother.

"Yes, Josie Segovia, it is a world that connects. I knew your great-grandmother when I was a little girl. How is Maria doing? She moved from Bruni, I heard, many years ago – so it has been years, decades since I've seen her. How is she?" Professor H asks.

"Well, she's getting old, and it's hard for her to get around," Josie answered.

How much did this young girl know? Nadine thought. Maria, to save her name and her family, had to vacate the house Nadine's father had bought her and move to another town. Nadine studied the picture. There she was, Maria Segovia – a fat, gray-haired old woman sitting on a wooden kitchen chair outside in the front yard with her large family.

The boys were now grown men, vaqueros. Standing tall with straw cowboy hats tilted back, they grinned at the camera, their worn boots peeking from their frayed Levi's 501 jeans. The handsome one, Aaron, was still handsome and dashing as a middle-aged man and still wore a red bandana knotted about his neck. The father, Mateo, sat proudly in front, and his sons and their wives, in homage, leaned toward him. Maria was slightly apart from all of them; one could have taken a pair of scissors and cut her away from the rest of the family without ruining the picture.

"What a lovely family you have, Josie," Professor H said. "How blessed you are."

Professor H started to say that it was a happy family, but she checked herself. Maria Segovia's face was not that of a happy woman.

"Thank you, Professor H. I think so too."

"Here, take the picture, place it next to your keyboard, and start writing. You can look at the picture to get more ideas for your essay," Professor H said.

"I think I'll try to write it without the picture," Josie said. "Is it okay to leave it with you on your desk for a while?" she asked.

So Josie knows, Professor H thought. Aloud, she said, "Yes, you may."

Josie went to her computer while Professor H walked among the students, peering at their computer screens and providing feedback to the students. When Professor H sat down at her desk to grade a few papers, she stopped midway and picked up the picture.

So this was her mother's best friend at one time and archenemy for always, Maria Segovia, she mused as she looked at the picture. Professor H nibbled on a bit of fresh mushroom and momentarily wound up in Bruni, Texas. Professor Nadine Hernandez thought:

> *Maria.*
>
> *Maria Segovia.*
>
> *Ahhh, Maria Segovia! With your dark eyes and your olive skin and your crude voice, you purred like a cat who's just finished lapping up cream from a saucer and who's just starting to curl up under some mesquite tree with my father.*
>
> *Ahhh, Maria! How tantalizing and intriguing you were! And how lonely and sad you are now.*
>
> *Ahhh, Maria! You taught me at age six what remains undisputed at age forty-six.*
>
> *Ahhh, Maria Segovia! What hard small breasts you had compared to Mother's soft, full breasts! You smelled of cheap perfume and Mother smelled tired.*
>
> *Ahhh, Maria! How your dark eyes flashed and danced and connived! And how Spanish dripped and rolled and trashed from your lips and throat! Oh, how you purred, arching your back, lowering your eyes, and curling your tongue!*
>
> *Ahhh, Maria! How my father pattered after you on alley-tomcat paws!*
>
> *You were happy then, Maria Segovia. You had Mateo, your husband, conveniently working on the Calaway Ranch, away for weeks at a time, and you had six – or was it seven? – mouths to feed, tugging at your hemline. These things made you happy and secure.*
>
> *But it was not these things that made you glow; it was the secret you had that made your eyes shine and your face flush and made all the other*

corncobs stuck up their asses, fake God-fearing women in Bruni whisper your name scornfully and wish inwardly and feverishly at the same time that they too could dare to do such a thing.

At age six, Maria, I watched that man, Father, with legs spread wide apart, sprinkle rose tonic on his coal-black hair, parting it carefully and crimping waves between his fingers. I watched him slap Old Spice on strong, healthy fair skin, and I watched him swagger out clothed in freshly ironed khakis – khakis my mother meticulously ironed – leaving her alone and the screen door halfway open.

Ahhh, Maria. So you too, like so many disappointed women, have grown fat, and your once-glossy black hair is now the color of the sage bushes that grow wild and never die on Father's ranch.

One rare moment, Maria, when I was sixteen, I walked down the alley, sandburs catching on my bobby socks, and knocked on your backdoor. I could see you and Father through the screen door. You were rolling tortillas on the white kitchen table that had been ours: Father's, Mother's, Janis's, Carolina's, and mine ever since I could remember. Then one day, it was gone.

Father is leaning back in a chair opposite you; he's gazing up into your face as if you were the Madonna with the long neck, and you are looking down and smiling at him. After a few moments, I creep away.

Ahhh, Maria. How the smells of fresh homemade tortillas trickled out the door and how the sounds of the Spanish language, your first language and Father's first language, strummed and conspired!

Ahhh, Maria. You must be seventy-six now – at least seventy six. And when was it that Mateo and your children packed your bags and moved you from that little house in Bruni to a little ranchito outside Hebbronville? It is there on that ranchito where you will live out your life missing my father and where you will know, but not hear, of the lingering death of my handsome lonely father.

Mother, with her fine auburn hair, grew old and fat too – but it was a lovely, untarnished old. And finally, when the time was right, she left Father to go and prepare the home, his boyhood home, for the only man she'd ever loved. Beneath the ebony tree, near Guerra, she waited for him. Father went back to her in October.

Ahhh, Maria. Your voice purred. Your eyes sparkled. Your back arched. At six and at sixteen, I learned from you. At forty-six, I spit. Fuck someone else's husband, and he's yours for life.

Like Alice, Professor Hernandez stops nibbling on the mushroom and sprouts back to her original size.

Professor H gets up and takes the photograph to Josie. "Don't forget your picture, Josie," she says.

THE BLUE SILK AFFAIR

Nadine got up from the bed where she and her husband were sleeping and walked down the hallway. She opened the hall closet and withdrew a fabric bag and then walked resolutely and quietly to the backdoor. She went into the garage, removed her cotton nightgown, and slipped on the blue silk dress she'd hidden earlier in the bag.

She slid into the Suburban and backed it out of the garage. At the corner of Thistlecroft and Pine Mountain, she stopped to pick up a man in jogging shorts. He was carrying a bag identical to the one from which she had taken the blue silk dress. He took off his shorts and put on the slacks that he, like Nadine, had hidden earlier in the bag. Neither spoke. Nadine drove through the night down Clay Road.

For a few miles, they drove in silence. Nadine blinked every time a car met them travelling in the opposite direction. The man, an enormous blond man, owned a construction company, and he was bored with his blond workaholic wife. Although she made a lot of money, and this he liked very much, he wanted to escape the mediocrity of married life. Nadine's eyes told him she felt pretty much the same way. His wife talked incessantly, blabbing about work and all the houses she'd sold, tossing her head back and blowing smoke rings in the air. Who did that anymore? She smelled of a sickening mixture of cigarettes and expensive perfume, and he found every excuse to "go for a little jog" mostly just to get some fresh air and to get away from her conversation. For god's sake, how many times had she mentioned to Nadine and Randall tonight at dinner that she was related to Katie Kristopher? Who cares if Katie Kristopher had made all those movies? Name-dropping bitch. And of course, she'd wanted Nadine and Randall to know that she was the one that made the big bucks, not him.

Nadine could smell the sweat from his body. Together their hearts pounded with the excitement. The chase had ended. She was a conquest: young and pretty with short dark hair that was cropped like a boy's. He had conquered her, standing close to her, looking down at her in his powerful way, making her feel small and delicate. And tonight he would claim the prize. The sweat beaded on his chest and trickled down to his flat hard stomach. The pants, he had left unfastened, for he was that sure of her. Those eyes during dinner practically fucked him when she happened to look at him. Nadine, both hands on the steering wheel, trembled slightly. Finally, she slowed down and pulled off on a side road. "I can't wait any longer," she whispered hoarsely.

He reached for her and pushed the blue silk dress up above her thighs with one hand, and with the other, he pulled his pants down. He rolled her onto her back and sank his weight on her. Nadine turned her head to avoid the stubble from his beard. The blue light from the Suburban's clock illuminated his strong long back and his firm tanned buttocks. She saw the clock.

"Oh god, Bret! It's midnight!" she wailed.

The Suburban turned into a damn pumpkin, and Nadine turned into a mouse.

Bret sighed and put on his jogging shorts. He put the pumpkin into the bag along with his slacks. He tried to put the mouse into the bag as well, but she squeaked and scurried into the woods. He looked an odd sight, jogging home with a pumpkin in his bag.

RANDALL'S DREAM

Nadine and her husband are driving to Office Depot to pick up folders for her literature classes.

Nadine's husband says, "Let me tell you about the dream I had last night."

Nadine yawns. She simply can't help it. She knows it's rude, but Randall's dreams are always so ordinary.

She says, "But don't you always dream about going to the grocery store or going to work?"

"Yeah, but not this time," he says, a little proud of himself.

"Okay. Tell me and then I'll analyze it," Nadine says a little unenthusiastically and thinks, *Analyzing dreams about work isn't exactly the most exciting thing. Of course, I suspect he leaves out a lot.*

"Well, it starts off in a gym. We're in this gym –"

"Who's *we*?"

"You and me."

"Is it a high school gym, or is it like a Gold's Gym?" Nadine asks.

"It's like a Gold's club." He slows down for a red light, drums his fingers on the steering wheel, and continues, "Anyway, we're in this gym, and we're sitting on a bench with ... uh ... uh ... some other people. Well, with another couple, I guess. Anyway, no one is saying anything. There's this big guy sitting next to us, and all of a sudden, you lean over and pull a hair off his chest."

"I do what?" Nadine asks incredulously. *But after all, it is a dream*, she thinks.

"You lean over and pull a hair off his chest. He's got this hairy chest. And you just reach over and pull a hair off his chest."

"Just *one*? Or a handful?" Nadine asks incredulously and a little teasingly.

"Just one. I guess," he says. And then he hurries on, "Anyway . . . um . . . uh . . . he says to you to pull your pants down so he can pull out one of your pubic hairs."

"What?" Nadine screams. *Doubly incredulous,* she thinks.

"He asks you to drop your pants, and you do. You push your pants down, and he leans over and pulls a pubic hair from you."

Nadine stiffens a bit. "He pulls one of my pubic hairs out?"

"Yep, he just leans over and pulls one of your pubic hairs out."

"And?" Nadine rolls her eyes upward. But he's driving, eyes on Mann road, and Randall doesn't see this, for he's stopping and speeding up.

"What does everybody do?" Nadine asks after a pause.

"Nothing," he says. "Nobody does nothing. Nothing."

"You mean you and . . ."

"I guess it's the man's wife or girlfriend . . . anyhow, no one does a thing."

"You mean everyone just sits there? Do they say anything? Do you? Or the man? Or the woman? Or me?" Nadine gushes.

"Oh, no one says anything. You pull your pants up, and we just sit there on the bench. Then the dream jumps to the next day or another day. I come home from work, and you are stepping into the shower. You have no hair on your pussy."

"What? Is it shaven?" Nadine asks.

"No, I don't think so. Anyway, I say to you, 'You let him pull your hair out.'"

"What?" Nadine shrieks.

"Yeah, there's no hair. None. I say again that you've let him . . . and then you say to me, 'But that's all we did . . . really . . . we just pulled each other's hair out. Nothing else happened.'"

He pulls into the darkened parking lot at Office Depot. It's about closing time, yet Nadine and Randall sit there for a bit.

Finally, her husband says, "That's the way the dream ends. You saying nothing else happened."

Nadine doesn't say anything; he too remains silent. *Why bother? Shovelful by shovelful, the dirt hits the coffin,* Nadine thinks.

Nadine reaches for the door handle, opens it, and states flatly, "That's a change from your dreams about work. I'll analyze it after we get the folders for my class."

She jumps down from the Suburban. The pavement's uneven, and she twists her ankle. "God damn it," Nadine mutters between clenched teeth. "Oh, god damn."

THE POEM IN YOUR POCKET DAY

The man looked at the woman with real envy. He tried to cover his envy, but he was unsuccessful. His deep-set, small green eyes became smaller and greener as he read the poem. The poem was not very long, yet it was astonishingly good. And she had written it in her American Lit class in about fifteen minutes! Randall believed it, for he had seen her sit down and, very quickly and without effort, write a story or a poem without fear and without show. She simply wrote with no regard for what people might say or think; what made it sickening to him was that some hidden aspect was revealed in her stories or poems so genuinely and, what was even more sickening, so insightfully! He tried to appear casual and nonchalant.

He said in an offhand manner, "So Poem in Your Pocket Day is on the same day as our anniversary?"

"Yes," she laughed delightfully.

"What exactly is Poem in Your Pocket Day?"

"Oh," she admitted, "I didn't know exactly what Poem in Your Pocket Day was either. It just happened to come up while I was checking my Yahoo e-mail, and there was this tidbit about Poem in Your Pocket Day, so I googled it to find out what it was. You basically take a poem you like and share it with people. But then, instead, I decided to write you a poem since I hadn't gotten you an anniversary present. And so I wrote it during class while the class was reading some of Langston Hughes and e-mailed it to you. I printed out a copy for you. So here it is. Here's your anniversary present," she said and laughed again.

She reached in her pocket and took out a loosely wadded ball of paper. She unfolded it and read the poem aloud, even though he had his iPad on his lap and obviously had his e-mail and the poem opened.

Nadine read in a half-mocking serious tone:

For Randall from Nadine

Oh. So.

This is Poem in Your Pocket Day.

This day is a poem.

A poem in a day for you and me.

A poem in a year for us.

A poem that's pocketed us tightly in faded blue jeans

still listening to Kristofferson's "Sunday Morning Coming Down"

and searching for our cleanest dirty jeans.

Oh. So.

On this day,

thirty-seven years ago,

during our lunch hour,

two novel poets,

you and I,

said, "I do."

I giggled throughout the day.

I'm giggling still,

crumpling up then smoothing out

the paper in my pocket.

She looked pleased with herself; this made the man even more detached than he previously was.

"Thirty-eight years ago," he corrected.

"Oh! Good golly, you're right! Thirty-eight years ago!" She laughed again. And then, after a few moments when he didn't respond, and with some embarrassment, she wadded up the paper again and stuck it back in her pocket. The man hit delete, and the poem disappeared from his inbox.

THE LAST MEETING

She stood in front of the mirror and watched as he stood behind her clumsily. Nothing happened. Fear clutched her throat. *Oh Jesus!* she thought. *Not again! What do you do? Smile coquettishly?* she asked herself. *Whatever a woman shouldn't do was evident – one didn't scoff and cry out, "Well, nothing's looking up today!" That'd end the relationship. One didn't shrug either and murmur, "Well, the relationship was pretty much so over." One also didn't pause, after a remark like that, and say, as the man looked glumly down, "This pretty much so cinches it."*

She speculated, teetering to and fro slightly on stilettos, *What's the next move? How do you save face? A man's ego – a man's life – was the crux here.*

She fiddled with the lace on the semi-teddy, some Victoria's Secret man-hooker she'd bought a few years back, and snatched from the lingerie drawer when he'd called. The black lace garter belt couldn't force the seams on the back of the sheer black hose to stay straight. It had been sheer agony bending over, easing the stockings up and over her calves and thighs, being ever so careful not to tear holes in the stockings with her nails, pushing the stockings out and over her curvy calves and thighs, looking backward in the full-length mirror in her bathroom, checking and rechecking to make sure the sheer stockings were straight and didn't have a run.

Now Dax rubbed his hands over her shoulders. *Jesus,* the woman thought to herself as she looked at their reflection in the mirror at her studio. His hands were rather soft. They were certainly much smaller than her husband's hands. She tossed her long wavy red hair slightly back and looked at him over her shoulder.

She pretended she didn't see the fear in his eyes.

Her eyes flashed. She thought, *My husband has Michelangelo hands.*

The man moved his incapable hands over the rhinestone straps then slightly down over the padded satin bejeweled brassiere. She felt nothing. Two inches of foam rubber acted as the chastity belt over her breasts. *"Now what?"* she asked herself. *What does a woman do? Say with casual condescension, "Oh, sweetie, it happens sometimes." Then add softly, "Perhaps another time?"*

Shit.

Billows of white floated around them. She felt as if she were tumbling lightly on billows and billows of cloudlike tumbleweeds. And then, before she could stop herself, she turned to face Dax and moaned, "Oh, what's the matter with me?"

FAIRY GODMOTHER BRINGS NADINE A BOX

The fairy godmother, Klimt's auburn beauty with Rubens's hued flesh, appeared before Nadine with a miniature box.

She waved her platinum wand studded with real diamonds, and gold dust – which smelled of nutmeg – misted down on Nadine.

At sixty-one, Nadine wasn't surprised or confused to see a fairy godmother in all her getup. Strange things happen in this world.

"Your mother sends you this box from heaven," the fairy godmother said.

Nadine still wasn't surprised. Explains the Klimt look – soft, tender white flesh, auburn hair like her mother's flesh and hair. It explains also the smell of nutmeg . . . like her mother's nutmeg cookies. The diamonds – pshaw! Nadine had worn her share of baubles.

Nadine takes the box, cradling it with both hands. She's still not surprised. She knows what's in the box. She's known since the first moment in her mother's womb when Nadine became female. And now her mother, many years after her death, is sending Nadine the box via fairy godmother Danaid Express.

Bio Poem

N. D. Etherly

N. D. Etherly
is a hidden hide,
a half-breed,
a ravishing reader,
a writhing writer,
a clay molder,
who's nobody.
N. D. wears scratched sunglasses,
old Levi's,
and real diamonds.
Born over a half century
ago in Laredo,
N. D. knows only Texas,
sometimes floats
from the Colorado River
to the Utley Bridge,
occasionally bumps by Bruni,
hails haute Houston from Herman Park,
visits old kings
and a new prince in San Antonio,
welcomes frail arms in Waco,
and visits underground ancestors,
(one a pure white Parisian),
past Javalina Road in Guerra.
A sage hunter,
living LustDust in Laredo,
N. D.'s nobody.
N. D. bends, struggles.
and makes an art of it,
hiding, that is.

CPSIA information can be obtained at www.ICGtesting.com
Printed in the USA
LVOW080822220213

321140LV00002B/74/P